DEATH LEAVES
THE STATION

DEATH LEAVES THE STATION

ALEXANDER THORPE

 FREMANTLE PRESS

AUTHOR'S NOTE

While the events in this story are fictional, the locations and historical context are not. I wish to acknowledge that this story is largely set on the traditional lands of the Yamatji and Noongar peoples, and that sovereignty of these lands has never been ceded. The ideas and prejudices of the characters often reflect attitudes which were especially prevalent in the early part of the twentieth century and have since been recognised as intolerant or harmful. I have included these in the interests of providing an accurate historical setting and in the recognition that the damaging legacy of racism should not be hidden or downplayed. No disrespect is intended.

To John, my grandfather, with thanks for the memories.

PROLOGUE

The house at Halfwell Station smelled of dust and dirt and heat.

It hulked over sparse grasses, a heavy thing of corrugated iron and jarrah forced into foreign shapes. Making no concession to the climate, the house had been fashioned from distant memories of Lancashire, a world away, and left to collect dust on the edge of the Western Australian outback. High, proud ceilings subjected the occupants to frigid winter months and summers of unbearable heat, while the wide hallways, built to be filled with the bustle of butlers and parlourmaids, made unwelcome echoes of even the smallest noise.

Through this hollow, half-sleeping world, on a dry November afternoon, three sharp knocks rang like the tolling of a bell.

The reverberations died away and after a long moment of silence, a series of answering sounds emerged from the heart of the house: the scrape of a chair on aged floorboards, the creaking of hardwood, the slow growth of unhurried footsteps.

Dull light swept into the hallway as the front door opened, bringing with it a hint of the dying day's heat. The lady of the house blinked out over the threshold to the grinning little man beyond.

'A very good evening to you,' he said, bobbing his head slightly.

Mrs Harris studied the caller.

He was clad in a singular brownish garment, something

like a cassock or shift, which fell almost to the ground, all but concealing the pair of battered sandals beneath. The man's face was warm, dark and weathered, shadowed by a slight beard and topped with a greying mop of curls. His eyes gleamed.

Beyond and behind him, the beaten dust stretched quietly to the horizon, punctuated here and there by stubble and scrubby stands of wattle.

There was no horse or vehicle in sight.

'I don't suppose I could trouble you,' the little man ventured, 'for a spot of tea?'

Following a moment's healthy hesitation, the front door swung wide to admit the stranger, then closed once more upon silence.

Somewhere in the mulga, a mile or two to the south, a corpse lay slowly cooling.

CHAPTER ONE

The stalwart landholders at Halfwell had weathered decades in their remarkable building. Through drought and dust, they continued to hack and scrape away at the unwilling earth, more from habit than from any real hope of a yield. Hardship hadn't yet deterred them; dwindling returns seemed unable to sap their strength.

The gold rush of the late nineteenth century had lured the Harrises to the region, and the reports of those who had braved the Great War convinced them that there was nothing to be gained from looking further afield than Mullewa—the town which had, at a distance of some thirty miles, the dubious distinction of being the station's nearest neighbour. Aside from the occasional rotation of roving stockmen and domestic hands, the appearance of a new face at Halfwell was a rare affair.

Neville Harris was not a little surprised, then, to arrive home to an extra setting at the supper table.

Having spent the afternoon repairing and re-tensioning one of the property's more remote boundary fences, he was sunburned, sore and coated from foot to fingers in tenacious red dirt. It was his custom, upon returning from the paddocks, to enter the house from the rear, where the kitchen door hung perpetually open to a stony courtyard, shaded slightly from the sun.

After seeing his horse fed, watered and stabled, he treated

his own face and palms to a cursory splash from the precious, stagnant water in the wash trough and staggered wearily inside. The long sideboard—usually laden with bread, cheese and a pitcher of cordial in anticipation of his return—was bare but the clink of cutlery from the adjacent dining room promised that his hunger would be short-lived.

The dining room was somewhat inaccurately named, as the Harrises and their sole daughter usually took their meals in the small chamber immediately adjoining the kitchen, while the maid, stock-hands and roustabouts ate together in the courtyard. The dining room was reserved for those relatively rare occasions on which they were graced with a guest—as was the case, Mr Harris intuited, on this particular evening.

Whatever his expectations had been—the station's intermittent visitors could include anyone from regional officials conducting land surveys to peripatetic tinkers and fugitives—the master of the house was clearly surprised by the sight that awaited him. Against the backdrop of the stately (if slightly musty) dining room, with its well-preserved fleur-de-lis wallpaper and finely detailed plaster coving, the mysterious visitor's earthy aesthetic was thrown into particularly sharp relief.

The little man leapt from his chair, coarse shift billowing as he bounced across the room to shake the hand of his host. Mr Harris took an involuntary step backwards, somewhat alarmed by the force of the man's enthusiasm, but recovered quickly enough to return the handshake.

As the subsequent silence began to loom, Harris turned to his wife.

'Aren't you going to introduce me to our guest?' he asked.

Ruth Harris was a short, wiry woman of early middle age. Her slightly greying hair was pulled up into a high bun, lifting her eyebrows into an expression of perpetual bemusement which had never seemed more suitable than in the present circumstances.

'That—that would be a little hard, love,' she stammered, somewhat apologetically. 'He hasn't got a name, you see.'

Neville Harris's gaze flickered from the eternally astonished face of his spouse to the visitor's benevolent grin and back again.

'Hasn't got a name?' he barked. 'Don't be ridiculous.'

This admonishment was directed, for some reason, at Mrs Harris but it was the visitor who answered.

'Ridiculous it may be,' he admitted, his smile unwavering, 'but your wife is quite right. I gave it up.'

Harris snapped round to stare at the little man in disbelief.

'Gave it up? Nonsense. What kind of man gives up his own name?'

Mrs Harris felt compelled to interject.

'A friar,' she said quickly, a note of warning in her tone. 'Our guest is a *man of the cloth*.'

'Ah.' Her husband gave a little cough, glancing at the gilt crucifix which hung above the door.

The friar's eyes sparkled.

'A pleasure to meet you, Mr Harris,' he laughed.

The three were seated, the teapot was lifted anew, and the conversation began slowly to find its feet, propelled by the potent combination of Earl Grey, shortbread and the grateful garrulousness with which Mrs Harris attacked any ambassador of the outside world. As she whittled away at the wooden silence, her husband looked the stranger up and down, waiting for a familiar pattern to emerge from the grain.

His name, it seemed, was not the only thing the man had given away.

In becoming a friar with one of the stricter mendicant orders, he had relinquished any claim to material wealth, all manner of fleshly pursuits and any semblance of personal vanity.

'The robe, of course, is the one exception I allow myself.' He winked, rubbing the coarse fabric between thumb and forefinger. 'Savile Row.'

Mrs Harris tittered. 'He's come all the way down from Beagle Bay,' she told her husband, eager to exhibit the information she had gleaned prior to his arrival. 'On a sort of pilgrimage, you see. He started at the Trappist mission house up there and walked most of the way down—walked! And you'll never guess where he's headed next ...'

The question of whether or not her husband could, in fact, guess the friar's next destination would never be satisfactorily resolved, as the period of time which elapsed between Mrs Harris posing the challenge and providing the answer was so small as to defy measurement by even the most accurate of chronographs.

'He's off to Mullewa to see old Father Hawes!'

At the mention of this name, the mendicant noticed Mr Harris's brow smooth from its erstwhile expression of mild dissatisfaction to something almost approaching a smile and moved to take full advantage of the fact.

'It is my understanding,' the friar said, 'that Monsignor Hawes has undertaken the construction of a church in the continental style. It's something that I would very much like to see, and—if at all possible—to help construct.'

Mr Harris dipped his head about a quarter of an inch in what was, for him, an almost emphatic expression of approval.

'A good man, Hawes,' he said, gruffly.

'He designed the cathedral they're building down in Geraldton,' his wife added, 'and he's working on the Mullewa place himself. The main building's done, but Hawes isn't. He's started on the priest house now, carting stones all about the place. Doesn't let it get in the way of his services, mind—even holds mass just out of town for the natives!'

As if on cue, there was a soft knock at the door and a young woman entered, carrying a tray laden with dishes which she began to arrange on the table with studied precision. The Harrises barely looked up but their guest jumped to his feet to greet her.

'Unless I'm very much mistaken,' he smiled, 'I believe I have the pleasure of addressing Miss Mariana Harris.'

He was indeed, as it transpired, very much mistaken.

Had the serving woman understood him, she would have laughed, but knowing only a few words outside of her native Wajarri—mostly related to the execution of simple domestic drudgeries—she merely acknowledged the young mistress's name with a shy smile and retreated to the kitchen, clutching the empty tray.

Puzzled, the mendicant looked to Mr Harris. 'Your wife mentioned that you had an adopted daughter,' he said. 'I simply assumed ...'

Mrs Harris laid a placating hand on her husband's tanned forearm. It was a few moments before the old farmer managed to attempt a smile.

'Think nothing of it,' he forced out.

'That was Daisy, the serving girl,' came Mrs Harris's hurried explanation. 'Our daughter, of course, is not a native. Her father was a Chilean, drawn to this country by the promise of gold—as were so many. It is my understanding that his wife was opposed to the move and followed in great distress, convinced that a terrible fate would befall them in some distant desert—and so it did.'

'We'd do best not to speak of it now,' put in Mr Harris in a low voice, inclining his head towards the wall opposite.

'Her room is just next door,' said Mrs Harris in a stage whisper. 'Don't want to distress the poor girl.'

'Will Mariana not be joining us for tea?' The mendicant's tone was mild but his eyes were keen over the rim of his cup— keen enough to catch the rapid, loaded look that passed between husband and wife.

'She will,' said Mrs Harris.

'She will not,' said Mr Harris, at precisely the same moment.

A fraught pause gripped the room, but only for a second—

the lady of the house was quick to capitulate.

'My husband is quite right, of course,' she said quickly. 'Our daughter has been ... somewhat indisposed this afternoon.'

'It saddens me to hear that,' the friar said. 'Nothing serious, I trust?'

Mrs Harris returned her cup to the saucer a little too carelessly, making the china ring like a cymbal in the silence. For the first time that evening, she seemed unwilling to speak, deferring to her spouse with an almost defiant turn of the head.

'Just a cold,' grumbled the farmer at last. 'She'll be right as rain in a day or two. We make 'em tough out here.'

Further efforts at conversation amounted to little, and the three presently set upon a subdued supper. The only communication of note from thereon in, aside from the utilitarian requests for salt and other condiments to be conducted about the table, dealt with the guest's refusal to try Mrs Harris's much-vaunted lamb chops. This he did politely but firmly, indicating that meat was another of the earthly vices he had vowed away. In doing so, the friar finally managed to alienate his sole known ally at Halfwell Station and from that point on, the lady of the house made no further pretence towards pleasantries.

Indeed, she exerted only a nominal effort to conceal her relief when, as dinner finally reached its end, the little man politely declined the offer of a bed for the night. Though her charitable Catholic soul did chafe sorely at the thought of anyone going without shelter—let alone a man of the faith—Mrs Harris knew that both she and her husband would sleep all the more soundly knowing that the itinerant friar lay without their walls; the guest himself cited a preference for sleeping beneath the open canopy of the stars.

Having provisioned him with flour and apples enough to see him to Mullewa, the Harrises indicated a small stand of eucalypts a half-mile distant as a suitable place to set up camp.

Their duty done, they retired unburdened to the starched comfort of their quarters while the mendicant traipsed away through the dust. Silence stole back through the dark to reclaim Halfwell Station, where it reigned until dawn, disturbed only briefly by the tired midnight protest of floorboards as an escape was effected.

CHAPTER TWO

Though the night was far from cold, a small fire crackled beneath the trees, describing a flickering sphere within which the mendicant sat, testing the knots of a hempen hammock. He hummed aimlessly as he worked, buttressed by the roots of an ancient salmon gum. Around him, the shadows ebbed and flowed, a scrimshaw scene of red and gold. At length, one shadow broke from the wavelike rhythm of its fellows and slid steadily towards the fire.

The mendicant looked up into the face of a young woman.

Her pupils were wide, seeming to swallow the firelight, and her cheeks pulled taut with the work of controlling some wild emotion. She was clad in an old nightdress, the hem of which had been pulled to the side and knotted just below the left knee so as to keep it from dragging in the dirt. Boots of worn leather, far too large, engulfed a good portion of each leg; they must have been taken from the verandah outside the door at the last possible minute. It was clear that her flight into the dark had not been the result of extensive planning.

The little friar looked the newcomer up and down before nodding at the fire.

'The billy's boiled,' he said calmly.

The woman's reply was so direct as to sound harsh.

'I didn't come here for tea.'

Her lips twitched for a moment afterwards, and the mendicant could see what a constant effort it was to keep her expression steady. He offered no response, merely setting aside his hammock and opening a hand towards the fire. The woman made no move to sit.

'You're a priest,' she said, heightened emotion placing the statement midway between a question and an accusation.

'Of sorts,' he replied. 'And you, I can only assume, are Mariana.'

Her dark eyes flashed.

'Ana,' she said, toying with the silver locket that hung from her neck. 'Just "Ana".'

Suddenly, whatever power had propelled her out into the night was finally and abruptly exhausted—snuffed out by the simple reality of speaking her own name—and she sank to her knees, staring into the fire. Something escaped with that name; something that left a girl sitting where a woman had been moments earlier, and the mendicant realised that she couldn't be much older than seventeen or eighteen.

He withdrew two tin mugs from his bag. Lifting the billy from the coals with a wire hook and a practised hand, he began to fill them.

Ana took the proffered tea without a word.

'I'm afraid I can't offer you any milk,' said the friar. 'It doesn't keep long in this heat.'

She raised one corner of her mouth in an automatic gesture of acknowledgement.

For a long time, the fire's ravenous crackle was the only sound. Setting aside his tea, the mendicant reached for the hammock and resumed his work, splicing and readjusting several of the outer strands.

'Do you take confession?'

The words escaped her lips in a rush before she clamped them shut, seemingly betrayed by her own small voice. For the first time, it was the mendicant who seemed to hesitate.

'You may tell me anything you wish,' he said at length, 'without fear of judgement or reproach. Your words will not reach any other. In all good faith, though,' he added, 'I cannot offer you absolution.'

Ana looked up, puzzled. 'Why?' she asked.

The friar kept his gaze fixed steadily on the strands he was splicing.

'In renouncing my name and position, I have also temporarily renounced my clerical office within the church. I am now a lay brother, no closer to the divine than the humblest among my fellow men—all of which means that I am no longer able to relay correspondence upstairs, so to speak.' The smile with which he accompanied this remark was a grim imitation of his customary carefree grin.

Ana regarded him quietly, her hand rising to the silver locket that hung beneath the faded lace collar of her nightgown.

'You're a runaway!' she gasped.

The erstwhile priest made no move to react or repudiate but Mariana had already made her decision. Her face was set with grim purpose once more but the fear that tugged at the corners of her eyes was gone. She drained her tea and stood.

'Come with me,' she said, quietly. 'I have to show you something.'

* * *

They walked in silence for the most part, Ana leading the way. Beyond the trees lay wide fields of stubble—testament to the volume of the recent wheat harvest—which gave way at intervals to small shrubs, balga and flannel bush. The sand was hard and cool, swallowing the sound of their footsteps. The slender moon hung low above the horizon, its meagre light more than matched by the wild, careless brushstrokes of the Milky Way as it arced across the southern sky. Soft clicks and rustles sounded occasionally from the surrounding darkness, hinting at the scurrying things that made the night their home.

'Not long now,' Ana said.

By the mendicant's reckoning, they had been walking for about twenty minutes. The set of the stars told him that they were travelling in a more-or-less southerly direction, but other than that, he could make out no obvious landmarks. Beyond the stubble, the scrub around them looked much the same as the landscape through which he had been walking for the past few weeks: dry, flat and open.

To Mariana Harris, evidently, things had a different hue. She stopped here and there to note indeterminate patches of desert grass, or stooped in passing to check a certain rock (how it differed from its thousands of reddish-brown brethren, the friar was unable to discern), making a small noise of approval as she did so. At one point, she paused to examine an improbable wreath-shaped clump of wildflowers, small and bright in the starlight, and seemed to steer slightly west as a result.

For the most part, however, their course stayed true.

Neither traveller made any overture towards conversation— the still night seeming to demand a reverential silence—but the mendicant noticed an increased agitation in his guide's movements as they progressed. Her breath grew shallow and ever sharper, her steps uneven; at times it seemed as if she were about to break into a run, while at others she slowed almost to a halt, as if afraid of what lay ahead.

Then, catching sight of a low tumble of stones rising suddenly from the sand, she stopped dead.

'Too far,' she mumbled, pulling at the sleeves of her nightdress. She spun on a sandy heel and set off in the direction they had come, breaking into a frantic run.

Only twenty yards later, she pulled up short.

'It was here,' she panted. 'He was *here.*'

With a panicked pirouette, she began to run back again.

'He?' asked the friar, taking a cautious step forward. 'My dear, I'm not exactly sure —'

He broke off as Ana dropped to her knees in the sand.

'Here,' she said again, and before the mendicant could press any further, he saw it.

The sand before them gave way to a low, haphazard row of stones, about two feet high and perhaps three times that in length. In the darkness, the mendicant could not discern much in the way of geological detail, but even the heavy curtain of night could not hide the swathe of blood which slicked the surface of the nearest stone, reaching darkly out across the sand.

'*Madre de Dios*, he was here,' Ana said. 'Just a moment ago, he was here.'

The friar peered past her into the gloom. Beyond the rocks, the sand was scuffed and furrowed. A series of irregular indentations—almost akin to the track of some strange beast— meandered about the rocks, mired at intervals by blood and shadows. The trail, if a trail it was, extended only a few feet before being swallowed up by the darkness.

Ana's voice was weaker now, an echo of itself. 'He's gone.'

CHAPTER THREE

Detective Sergeant Arnold Parkes hated his moustache.

In this, he was not alone: his wife, his children and a sizeable majority of the Geraldton Police Force were united in silent, solemn hatred of the twisted thing that squatted atop his upper lip.

He had first decided to omit the razor from his morning ablutions some five years ago, a particularly dashing and hirsute figure in a cigar advertisement having caught his eye at a time when the approach of middle age rendered him vulnerable to impulsive behaviour.

Six hours into the experiment, he knew he'd made a mistake.

Sitting over scones and jam in the tearoom beside the station, he squinted at his feebly budding bristles in the back of a polished spoon and resolved to shave the very moment he reached home.

To the eternal detriment of all involved, however, Detective Sergeant Parkes had the great misfortune to be saddled with a uniquely supportive and loving wife; a devoted woman whose practised tact remained steadfast even when faced with the grisly and unexpected growth slowly annexing the lower portion of her husband's face.

Not wanting to damage his pride—which she knew to be a fragile thing—she imbued her show of support with altogether too much fervour. So powerful, in fact, were her torrents of enthusiastic verbiage and overtures of wild admiration that Parkes came quickly to believe that shaving could well deal his wife a serious emotional blow.

The upshot of all this was that for half a decade, both parties had devoted considerable reserves of energy to maintaining the pretence that the moustache didn't make them want to scream, each believing that their stoic endurance of the thing was a moral and matrimonial sacrifice made for the benefit of the other. In a strange way, it brought them together; they baulked at it through breakfast, loathed it at lunch and despised it at dinner. When his profession required him to shuffle papers at the precinct or make his rounds through the streets of Geraldton, his wife's share of the work was gladly taken up by fellow officers or passers-by, who would often cast alarmed glances at the moustache or absent-mindedly raise a hand to their own lips in mute sympathy. It was not uncommon for Parkes to catch the odd whispered word in passing, often featuring topiary as a theme.

Even on a day such as the one in question, when cases of a criminal nature called him away to fulfil his duties in a less quotidian context, the moustache never failed to arouse enormous feeling in those who were faced with it. Thankfully, the small crowd assembled at Halfwell Station to greet the detective sergeant had a ready-made excuse for the discomfited expressions that passed between them: the grim spectre of death.

* * *

Under normal circumstances, Parkes would not have been called this far from the coast.

Mullewa was equipped with its own small police station, single-roomed but serviceable, which admirably handled the town's small, relatively predictable criminal element. Drunk roustabouts, truculent miners, claim-jumping and petty theft were the usual fodder of the Mullewa police, and the three constables who comprised it had so far proved more than sufficient. Of course, violent crime was not unknown—the town being a rather remote settlement, with all the requisite ills thereof—and there were several murders on record. Though brutal, they were easily explained: base, ugly crimes of passion or possession. The matter at hand, unfortunately, did not fall within the realm of normal circumstance or, to put it in the words of the esteemed detective sergeant:

'There's not a single lick of sense in the whole bloody story!'

Shading his eyes with a meaty hand, he squinted over the sand once more.

In the full, fierce light of day, the scene was certainly clearer but the actual events of the previous forty-eight hours remained just as obdurately obscure. A lone set of tracks—commensurate with a single horse and a simple, two-wheeled sulky—crept across the scrub from somewhere to the north, only to be trampled and scuffed into nothingness a few metres from where Parkes now stood. Something like a trail surfaced again some yards to the south, but only at intervals. To complicate matters further, it seemed to split into two, and sometimes three, dispersing and being reunited several times before finally vanishing for good.

The stone, at least, had not disappeared. The blood which stained its surface was now a dun, sullen brown, the surrounding sand cracked and muddied in curious ridges that could—with a willing eye and the ready application of an artistic imagination—be said to form the outline of a neck and a shoulder.

Of the body itself, however, there was not the slightest sign.

* * *

It was the rummiest tale to come ringing down the telegraph wires since the Great War, thought Parkes. A man is discovered on the edge of the desert, lying dead in a pool of his own blood, miles away from anywhere. Less than twenty-four hours later, he vanishes completely, with no apparent effort being made to either clean up or conceal the crime and nothing in the way of footprints or wheel ruts nearby. To top it off, there are no reports of anyone going missing from any of the surrounding towns or settlements and no reason whatsoever for a man of any description to be wandering around this far-flung corner of the country in the normal course of affairs, especially in the wee hours of the morning.

'Who found the fellow?' demanded Parkes, rounding on the small group clustered behind him.

As one, heads turned towards Mariana, but it was Neville Harris who answered. As the sole male in permanent residence at Halfwell Station, he operated under the assumption that he was the target of all conversation, unless otherwise specified.

'My daughter found him,' he growled.

Parkes nodded. He knew this already, having been informed in the course of the initial dispatch, and again on arriving at the station. His investigative technique—which had all the subtlety of a tenderising mallet—was simply to hammer his suspects with the same questions over and over again until cracks began to form in their stories. Unfortunately, as with every other aspect of this singularly trying case, the possible identity of the murderer remained, at present, remarkably opaque.

Stroking the bisected broom beneath his nostrils, he cast his eyes across the small assembly.

The girl was the only one who had actually laid eyes upon the body but her age, frame and femininity would have made it difficult for her to draw blood from a man, let alone leave him stone-dead and drag his body off to God-knows-where. Even if she had managed to pull the deed off, with the aid of accomplice or accomplices unknown, why would she then go back and raise the alarm?

Then there was the friar.

Though Parkes was staunchly C of E, he harboured an automatic, ingrained respect for any man pursuing a Christian calling, regardless of denomination. This particular man, however; well, he thought, it's awfully difficult to trust a chap with no name, that's all—especially one who happens to pop out of the wilderness like a madman on the very same day a murder occurs. Regardless of anything else, the mendicant's constant, loony grin was almost enough to have him thrown into a cell.

Still, Parkes had to concede with some reluctance, it was the friar who had made the thing known. Were it not for his insistence and initiative, the landowners may well have found it more expedient to simply shrug off the mystery and save themselves the nuisance and notoriety of an official investigation.

The only remaining suspects, then, were the owners of the property themselves. Mrs Harris, once again, had the obvious handicap of her sex but she could perhaps have acted in concert with another. Parkes watched the little woman wringing her pink hands; she certainly seemed nervous, but this could be attributed with equal ease to the sickly presence of death, the official awe of entertaining a high-ranking officer from the coast or simply the rare and overwhelming experience of having two visitors in as many days.

And Mr Harris?

Parkes wondered. Harris was clearly a man capable of great anger; now, as he stared at his daughter, his face was reddened by much more than sun. Could he have killed someone? Or killed to protect someone? Surely, though, he would've gone to more effort to conceal the evidence, especially given that the crime took place on his property.

There were a few native fellows standing about, too—roustabouts, mostly, and other hired hands. They stood clustered together, silent and expressionless, a few yards behind their employers. Parkes had noticed a couple of others by the homestead, a serving girl and an old bloke hanging around the stables, but he felt fairly confident in saying that if an indigenous fellow had been the one to do the deed, he would've had the sense to clear off, quick smart. The poor beggars had enough to fear from white justice when innocent; it was more than their lives were worth to risk raising a hand to the colonisers.

'When was the body found?' asked Parkes.

Again, it was Mr Harris who answered. 'Night before last,' he muttered. 'Some hours before dawn.'

'And what, might I ask, was your daughter doing wandering all over the country in the middle of the night?'

Though in third person, the question was directed squarely at its subject. She lifted her eyes for the first time, and the detective sergeant was surprised to note that they were clear and dark, unreddened by tears, unwidened by fear. She stared at him for several long seconds, saying nothing.

'Several reasons spring to mind for a young lady to go walking in the wee hours,' Parkes went on. 'None are particularly wholesome.'

'I was looking at the stars,' said Ana, defiant.

Parkes looked to her parents for confirmation, receiving a grudging nod from Mr Harris.

'She's managed to get hold of a book on constellations,' the farmer said. 'Floats around at all hours of the night now, gawping up at the sky. Not the sort of thing I'd encourage, you understand, but her mother claims it's educational.'

A tense series of looks passed between man and wife, indicating that the surface of a long-running dispute had been scratched. Parkes hurried to resume control of the conversation.

'What drew you to this area in particular, Miss Harris?'

Ana opened her mouth to reply, only to be interrupted by her father.

'Now look here,' Harris said. 'That's enough. This is my property, you know —'

'A fact that does nothing to distance you,' the officer cut in, sternly, 'from the seriousness of a crime that may well have been committed where we now stand. I am treating this as a murder investigation and you would do well to let that investigation run its course. Any failure to cooperate will be treated as an obstruction of justice, with all the requisite penalties thereof.'

After a moment or two of taut deliberation, Mr Harris cursed quietly and stepped back, leaving Parkes to twirl his moustache in satisfaction. He considered himself—quite wrongly—to be a fair, equable man but could not deny the joy to be had in the occasional show of officious force.

At that moment, an indigenous tracker appeared, leading a piebald horse.

'No more sign of 'im, boss,' he said in a deferential voice. 'No body, neither.'

'How far did you go?'

'Good few miles. Nothing there.'

Parkes adjusted his jacket haughtily. 'Thank you, Cooper. Get back to the homestead and see what the other natives have to say.' He smiled thinly at the Harrises. 'Perhaps our hosts would be so kind as to escort you.'

Without so much as nod, the tracker turned to comply, but the others were less eager to take their leave.

'What about my daughter?' asked Mrs Harris.

Parkes looked at the girl, and past her to the mendicant.

'I shall require these two for a little while longer,' he said. 'I feel confident that they will oblige me by taking me through exactly what they saw here.'

Ana was first.

'To begin with,' said the detective sergeant, with pen poised over notebook, 'I'll be needing your full legal name.'

The girl took a deep breath and, fixing her inquisitor with the sort of careless, contemptuous look that only someone in their teen years can truly muster, reeled off a staccato storm of

Latinate appellations. Parkes managed to rush his pencil halfway through the first word before sputtering to a halt.

'One at a time!' he barked.

With only the barest hint of a smile, the young lady obliged.

'Mariana,' she said, slowly, 'Constanza, de Azevedo —'

Parkes began on a new line.

'Y de Meneses —' Ana paused, giving the officer time to cross the uprights and close the loops in his careful cursive, before adding, with exaggerated precision: '*Harris*.'

Parkes grunted.

Though still far from cosmopolitan, Western Australia in 1927 was no stranger to distant civilisations: the gold rush had brought treasure-seekers from as far afield as Argentina, Peking and the Caucasus, while the state's north-western corner relied on the skill of pearl divers from Japan and camel drovers from all corners of the orient.

More recently, the receding tides of war and resource depletion had left human flotsam of every description scattered about the state and a continental name was no longer the subject of eyebrow-raising novelty. Having confined the unruly thing to paper, Parkes seemed content to pay it no further heed, merely silencing the friar—who had been murmuring the syllables of Mariana's name in a meditative fashion—with a sharp glare before pressing onwards.

'Your age?'

'Nineteen in March.'

'Why don't you begin, Miss Harris, by telling me precisely what compelled you to leave your quarters the night before last?'

'I couldn't sleep,' she replied, 'so I went out to look at the stars.'

Plausible enough—the darkness creeping in below her eyes bore testament to Ana's lack of sleep. As an excuse, though, the officer found it deeply unsatisfying, perhaps because the night in question had been more than a little overcast. He made a note to return to this point later in the interview.

'At about what time did you leave the house?'

'Between half past ten and eleven thirty,' said Ana, after a moment's thought.

'You're quite sure of that, are you?'

'More or less.' A sharp look from the detective sergeant informed her that greater exposition was required. 'My father usually retires at nine,' she went on, 'and mother reads for an hour or two in the sitting room before following him. I didn't take my leave until well after they were both in bed.'

Parkes made a note to have the girl's parents corroborate the timing.

'It is customary, then,' he went on, 'for you to go gallivanting about the place in the middle of the night, is it? Stargazing?'

'It's very calming,' replied Ana.

Finding further details unforthcoming, Parkes changed tack. 'By which door did you make your egress?'

'I climbed out of my bedroom window,' the girl said, as plainly as if she were discussing the previous night's supper.

The detective sergeant paused, tapping his pencil in a distracted tattoo. He regarded his subject anew.

She wore a long, modest dress of light cotton, far from new, but clean and skilfully mended. The sleeves were rolled back to show slender wrists—by no means weak, but surely not possessed of the strength to end a man's life. The girl's features were dark, her skin the mild, even hue typical of her Hispanic origins. She wore her hair back in a loose bun from which errant curls sought to escape at every opportunity.

The overall picture, in the professional opinion of Detective Sergeant Parkes, was not one of a murderer, but there was certainly something disquieting in her manner and, without a doubt, a great deal of information being withheld.

The process of obtaining a full statement was prolonged by Ana's considerable reticence: she spoke as if rationing syllables and Parkes found himself asking twice the usual quantity of questions to receive only half the information. In the interest of preserving narrative momentum, however, the finished account of Ana's movements—as pieced together by the esteemed detective sergeant—is given here:

The young woman had climbed out of her bedroom window at least half an hour before midnight. The night had been calm and fairly cool, with no breeze to speak of. A canopy of clouds squatted atop the sky, darkening the stars and dampening the moon's second-hand light. Ana went first to the stables; taking a horse would produce too much noise, but there was a quiet pleasure to be had in visiting the gentle creatures. At this point, she felt confident that everyone else at the station was asleep— the gas lamp in her parents' bedroom had been extinguished long ago, and all sound from the shed where the servants slept had ceased. She did hear something outside—something like the creak of a gate—but a quick glance through a gap in the stables' wooden walls afforded a full view of the fence around the back paddock of the house, and there was no sign of man or beast.

'It may seem barren now, in the heat of day,' allowed the young narrator, gesturing to the dry, reddened earth at the detective sergeant's feet, 'but when we lie down to sleep, there are all manner of little things that creep out to take their turn at life. People think it silent, but the night out here is full of noises.'

'"Sounds, and sweet airs",' the little friar cut in, '"that give delight and hurt not."'

'You keep your nonsense to yourself,' said the detective sergeant. 'I'll get to you in a moment.'

'It's from *The Tempest*,' Ana pointed out.

'I know it is!' snapped Parkes, who didn't. 'Get on with it.'

Bidding goodnight to the horses, Ana had gone out into the paddocks, heading south-west. She picked her way carefully through the sharp wheat stubble to one of the little banked runnels which afforded a relatively straight path through the fields. Having made it past the wheat, she walked on without a destination in mind, moving through the dark in meditative silence. She knew the Harris property intimately—she had spent her whole life exploring it—but the further she wandered, the more the night seemed to tighten around her like a shroud, and the familiar landscape of her home became queer and foreign. The deepening shadows made hillocks and valleys of the slightest ripple in the sand, landmarks disappeared and distances became deceiving. Ana still knew where she was, but she could no longer fully trust her senses. By her estimation, it was now roughly an hour after midnight, and she was in a little-used stretch of fallow ground between two fields.

She was walking towards a low wall of stones—something that she had once believed, in the hazy breadth of childhood, to be the ruins of a faery castle, but which she now knew to be the remains of an abortive attempt at shaft mining. When gold fever struck Western Australia, very few people had been spared, and even the stodgy Neville Harris had tried his luck in the hope of getting a little more from his land. Finding only dirt beneath dirt, however, he had quickly filled in the shaft and gone back to his wheat and horses. The small pile of stones now served primarily to mark a stretch of dry creek bed which, being unfenced and otherwise fairly light on features, was often used as a less circuitous alternative to the main road by those travelling directly from station to station. More than that, though, the stones functioned as a general-purpose landmark, something on which to set one's sights in the largely homogenous patchwork of paddocks and grazing land. On their days off, the servants might lay a picnic lunch over the wider stones, while roustabouts often used them to describe the bearings of errant livestock—'three loose ewes headed west of the stones'.

Ana could now see the stones bulging blackly against the dim horizon and, through nothing more than force of habit, began to make her way towards them. Gradually, she became aware of the sound of hooves; distant, at first, and so faint that she thought she was imagining it, but growing slowly louder. The horse was heading in her direction.

'Horse?' Parkes pressed for clarification. 'Just the one?'

'I believe so.' Ana tossed her hair, as if to shake off the interruption, and plunged onwards.

There had been something else, too; the creak of wheels and wood. The horse was pulling a sulky, a little two-wheeled carriage. Ana couldn't see it, but she knew the sound—motor cars were still something of an indulgence in the Murchison region, and the need to keep them serviced and fuelled meant that a good deal of trade and transport was still conducted on the backs of beasts.

Not wishing, she said, to make the acquaintance of a stranger in the middle of the night, Ana hunched and hurried onwards, taking cover behind the stones.

'Miss Harris?' Parkes prompted.

Ana had lapsed into silence once more, but where her previous pauses had come across merely as sullen and somewhat recalcitrant, the detective sergeant now observed that his charge had begun, almost imperceptibly, to shake. Tension pressed the colour from her lips, and her eyes chased some vague, invisible thing into the middle distance.

'What did you see, Miss Harris?'

She turned a whitened face towards her interlocuter.

'*Nothing,*' she said. 'I couldn't see a thing. The horse drew closer, steadily closer, and louder—almost deafening! I thought that the thing would surely come upon me, and I would be trampled.'

Crouched behind the rock, the girl had simply screwed her eyes shut and prayed, waiting for the danger to pass. The hooves grew louder and louder still, until Ana could take no more. She swivelled and leapt up, ready to throw herself out of the sulky's path, when she was struck and paralysed by a sudden, brilliant flash of light.

'A storm?' pressed the detective sergeant. 'Lightning, was it?'

As the words left his lips, though, he realised it couldn't be the case. The early-summer storms which occasionally swept the region were both hotly anticipated and diligently recorded, bringing as they did the near-mythical promise of rain. The last storm had passed through weeks earlier, and no sign of further relief had yet been sighted on the broad, dusty horizon.

'It was an electric lamp,' said Ana. 'It must've been. The light was far too bright for an oil-flame and flashed on so suddenly— it could only have been ignited with a switch.'

To hear the young woman tell it, the flash had been as bright as the noonday sun. Her eyes, so long in darkness, had been dilated to the greatest possible extent, and the sudden light hit her hard. She was blinded for a full few seconds, confusion quickened by the searing pain of exposure. Senses whirling, she fell backwards into the dirt, gulping lungfuls of dust.

This blind, grimy tumult blighted the girl's testimony. She could not say how long she lay in the sand, nor attest with any real confidence to the events that had taken place around her. Only a single thing had imprinted itself on Ana's memory, and it had done so with all the scorching force of a branding-iron: in the same fevered instant the light had struck her, a man's voice rang out through the dark, raw and howling. It was a mere monosyllable, but to Ana, it seemed to echo across the sand for an eternity.

'What was the word?' urged Parkes, unable to keep his knuckles from whitening around his pencil.

Mariana Harris again met the police officer's gaze but all the prior poise had drained from her face.

'*Die*,' she whispered.

* * *

33

The rest of the girl's testimony was postponed slightly, the detective sergeant deeming it necessary to call an intermission for the sake of his young subject's nerves. In the absence of any adequate natural shelter, Parkes and his two witnesses retreated to the shade of the half-covered cart which had conducted them from the homestead. A steel canteen was recovered from the canvas saddlebag; the water inside, heated to just below scalding point by the steady sun, was nonetheless gratefully received by everyone in the party.

After a few minutes, throat soothed and nerves rested, Ana managed to move on with her narrative, describing how she had lain tight-curled behind the rock for an indeterminate length of time, hands clamped over her ears and eyes shut tight, waiting to feel the cold, inevitable kiss of a knife sliding between her ribs or the muzzle of a pistol pressed to her temple.

Instead, there was nothing.

When she gathered the courage to uncover her ears, all she could hear was the dull sound of hooves receding into the distance. Her assailant had gone. The breath left her in a terrible, choking sigh, and she let herself fall back on to the warm sand.

Warm and wet.

She had plunged her hand into a fresh pool of blood.

The horror still shone in her eyes as she described the body— the body she had lain beside for God-only-knows how long, as close as newlyweds on a honeymoon bower. The man had been pale and longish, of perhaps early middle age. He wore a short, full beard, and his eyes had been blessedly closed beneath thick brows. The wan moonlight made an accurate assessment of his hair colour difficult to arrive at, but Ana guessed it to be auburn or light brown—definitely not black, at any rate— more or less straight, and cut fairly short in length. His head was pillowed lightly upon the rock in a sickly simulacrum of sleep, while blood pooled and whorled in the gentle curve of his neck and soaked into the stiff fabric of his shirt.

'Must've been a head wound,' mused Parkes. 'They tend to bleed like the dickens. What was the man wearing?'

Ana shook her head a little, struggling to remember details which had seemed so secondary and insignificant at the time.

'A collared shirt, I think—white, or lightish, at any rate.' She closed her eyes briefly. 'A coat and braces, I suppose. Boots. Dark trousers.'

'Not a uniform, then?'

'I don't think so.'

There was a moment of silence. Parkes dropped down from the cart and stalked over to circle the rock, still silent and unedifying in the baking light of midday. Ana watched him, though it was clear from her abstracted expression that her thoughts were elsewhere.

A sudden question from the cart made them both jump; the friar had been so silent that they had almost forgotten him.

'Was the man dead?' he asked.

Parkes whipped round to face him.

'What on God's earth do you mean, man?' the officer snapped. 'He was lying in a pool of his own blood!'

'It's not a custom often cultivated by the living, I'll admit,' conceded the friar, 'but what if he'd simply been stunned? He may have regained his senses later and stumbled off into the bush.'

Parkes scuffed his heel in the sand. 'Either way,' he said, 'the poor fellow's dead now. He wouldn't have got far, having lost that much blood, and there's nothing in the way of shelter or water the whole thirty miles between here and Mullewa.' He tugged idly at his moustache. 'Still, it would throw a different light on things. Did you check him for a pulse?'

This last enquiry was directed at Ana, who shook her head.

'I had almost gathered up the courage to reach out and touch him when I heard something.'

With astonishing speed, the notebook reappeared. 'What was it?'

'I don't know,' Ana confessed. 'I was in no fit state to think clearly, you must remember. I heard movement and suddenly all that I could call to mind were the crazed murderers in my mother's penny dreadfuls, or the wild dingoes you hear about in the Western deserts, or the hairy people in the native tales the servants used to spin.' She sniffed. 'But I'm no heroine, it seems— my courage failed me utterly, and I ran as soon as I could find my feet. I ran the whole way home, not daring to stop until the window was bolted behind me.'

Parkes pondered a moment, then turned to the mendicant. 'You will attest to the fact that the body was missing when you arrived last night?' He waited to receive a nod before continuing. 'The killer must have returned, then, or an accomplice. A fellow doesn't simply die for a day or two and then get up and wander about.'

'One specific example does spring to mind,' noted the holy man wryly, but Parkes had already moved on.

'What did your father say when you told him about the body?' he asked Ana.

The girl looked at him for a moment or two without speaking, both hands clasped over her locket in a strangely childish gesture. Then, tellingly, she averted her eyes.

Parkes gave a start, his whole body stiffening like a terrier on the trail. Before he could speak further, though, the mendicant laid a brotherly hand upon his shoulder.

'I believe that I was the first to be made aware of the situation,' the friar said, gently.

'Twenty-four hours!' the detective sergeant growled. His eyes narrowed in disbelief, casting about from left to right in time with the furious workings of his mind. The friar, for his part, merely smiled.

'Miss Harris had undergone a considerable shock, as I'm sure you'll agree —'

'Shock is one thing, but this is altogether harder to swallow,' snapped Parkes. 'A whole day and night, and not so much as a peep! What's more, as you yourself have just noted, our man may very well have still been alive.' He spun in the sand, voice rising, to face his subject once more. 'Which would bestow upon you, Mariana Harris, a measure of the responsibility—however small or indirect—for his death!'

The accused made no move to defend herself; indeed, she made no move at all. The mendicant readied himself to reply in the young woman's defence but Parkes had already struck out for the cart.

'Come along!' the officer barked, clambering up to sit on the broad driver's bench. 'We're finished here.'

The others were wary of the detective sergeant's temper but warier still of the weary walk back to the homestead; they hesitated only a moment before following.

Creaking in the dusty silence, the cart set off.

CHAPTER FOUR

Though the afternoon was still fiercely hot, Parkes managed to cool down somewhat on the journey back to the house. By the time the cart pulled up outside the gate, the policeman had regained a good measure of the moderation which had seen him through fifteen years on the force, and when he finally took his seat in the dining room, he did so with composure fully restored and his slow rage yoked and cloistered.

As the tea was poured, Parkes cast a careful eye about the room. It was the first time he had actually been inside the house at Halfwell Station. The place was well appointed, certainly, the general layout and decoration being something of which Parkes thought his wife would approve, and she was seldom wrong on matters of taste; the sole exception to this rule drooped soggily into his tea as he took a careful sip.

There was a low hardwood cabinet running the length of the southern wall, upon which was arranged a collection of the sort of objects one might expect to see advertised in the more respectable monthly magazines: a delicate imitation-Delft dining set, a pristine cut-class decanter and a silver tea tray inscribed with a verse commemorating the coronation of Edward VII. A single painting hung on the wall opposite the door, the room's solitary concession to the visual arts: a rather unremarkable moorland idyll rendered in oils. Set in a small, brass-edged frame, the scene swam awkwardly in the centre of a wallpapered expanse, with only the opposing crucifix for company.

The detective sergeant lost himself for a moment in the indistinct oils, wondering idly if the gentle hills and vague greenery reflected the provenance of the Harris family. He'd heard of them before, of course—very little in the region escaped the notice of the constabulary—but nothing beyond the basics of location and profession. A smattering of northern vowels could be detected in the speech of both husband and wife but little else was immediately obvious. Further information would have to be won.

'This is a beautiful house,' said Parkes, fixing his hostess with what, in the absence of his moustache, might have come across as a disarming smile. 'But you've managed to make it a beautiful home, too. It must have taken some years—how long have you been in the area?'

Ruth Harris beamed, unmindful of the question's clumsy thrust. Before she could reply, though, her husband's gruff voice cut through the room.

'Ninety-one, we came in,' he blustered, proudly. 'Before the rush. Before the railway, even. Nothing but dirt back then.'

The interruption was no great shock to the others seated around the table. For the last quarter of an hour, Neville Harris had made it abundantly clear that the detective sergeant's questions would be answered only at his leisure, and had honed the pre-existing habit of speaking over his wife and daughter to an art form. He had even managed to wrestle the right of response from the friar on one or two occasions. Reduced for the most part to a spectatorial role, the other three swung their collective attention back and forth from interviewer to interrupter. Ana and the mendicant watched with some apprehension, the policeman's recent outburst still fresh in their minds, but the man himself seemed eerily undeterred.

'Disembarked at Geraldton, I suppose?' Again, Mrs Harris

was the target of the detective sergeant's question. 'I would've been new to the area myself, back then.'

The spectators Wimbledoned round automatically to look at Mr Harris but he showed no sign of interrupting again. After a few moments of silence, Ruth retrieved her smile.

'Actually, we came in at Fremantle,' she said. 'The place wasn't much to look at, to tell the truth. Rough and salty, with that awful prison squatting over the town.' She paused to fortify herself with a sip of tea, and her husband finally swept in.

'Awful place!' he decreed. 'Sodom-by-the-sea! Sots and sailors; all sorts of wretched, miserable folk. I'll never forget the blighter who made off with my watch at the Federal Hotel—brazen little devil climbed right in through the smoking-room window.' He shook his head. 'We were glad to see the back of that place, I can tell you—never had the slightest desire to go back.'

Ruth Harris nodded her silent affirmation, and the detective sergeant chipped in with some similarly disparaging remarks on the moral state of things down in the south-western corner of the country.

The mendicant watched the exchange with silent curiosity; if Parkes was so keen to get to the bottom of things, why was he pursuing such banal pleasantries? Mr and Mrs Harris seemed content enough to chatter away, while their daughter's apprehensive expression had gradually given way to a sort of perplexed boredom. As the conversation continued, though, and the policeman led his hosts northwards on a route of remembrance, the friar detected a subtle shift in the conversation. While the narrative crept closer to the present day, Ana was drawn in alongside her mother as an object of questioning once more.

Suddenly, the friar saw it: Parkes was only addressing himself to the female members of the family, starving Mr Harris of the attention to which he felt so manifestly entitled. Parkes was playing his subject with all the skill of a master fisherman, encouraging the old farmer to interject again and again, with growing frustration and dwindling care.

Then came the net.

With no concession to the continuity of the conversation, Parkes turned casually towards the youngest Harris and asked: 'When did you tell your father about the body?'

The girl froze, a hand flung up to her heart as if to prevent it from breaking the confines of her chest. For a mute, anguished moment the tableau held, and time seemed to stop—in reality, though, it was less than a fraction of a second before momentum carried Neville Harris into speech.

'Last night, about one o'clock.' He brought himself up short, glancing about the table as if wondering how he'd got there.

The room roiled with the silent churning of minds, each working to reconcile this revelation with their own understanding of events. Ruth Harris looked confused; Parkes wore an expression of slight surprise, while Ana's suddenly sweat-sheened face spoke volumes.

The mendicant, for his part, was impressed. He had pegged the old policeman as something of a staid fool, full of bluster and self-importance, but that question had been a work of art— Parkes had spotted a weakness and worried at it, widening it into something workable. Had he asked Harris directly, suspicion would've made the man pause. Had he attempted to hide that all-important query in a cavalcade of similar demands for detail, caution would've prepared Ana to pre-empt her father, who was now scrambling to regain control of the situation.

'Well, she'd had one hell of a shock, of course,' he said, hurriedly, 'and the female mind can be a very delicate thing, as I'm sure you know. You heard the story—my daughter was lucky to get away with her life! Had to spend the whole day in bed, white as a sheet. She could hardly speak—how could she begin to tell me something like that?'

The detective sergeant sat impassive behind his moustache.

'And really,' Harris ploughed onwards, 'what good would it've done? I took the horse out to look for the bloke as soon as I heard, and a couple of the lads with torches—just like I told you, remember? Didn't find a trace!'

'You neglected to divulge the fact that your search only began a full day after the fellow's death,' said Parkes, 'a fairly pertinent point, the omission of which must be considered nothing less than a deliberate attempt to subvert the course of my investigation—and by extension, the cause of justice.'

Panicked by the officer's lengthening prosody, Harris changed tack.

'I was only trying to protect my little girl,' he protested, glancing for the first time at his daughter. 'I thought it might look bad for her if you knew.'

The policeman raised an eyebrow. 'It looks an awful lot worse now,' he pointed out. 'And I'm afraid she isn't your little girl.'

Mr Harris stopped short, looking as if he'd just stepped into the path of a freight locomotive.

This time, it was his wife's turn to cut in. 'What on earth do you mean by that?' she demanded, a note of anger creeping into her voice.

'What I mean,' the officer explained, allowing a superior smile to rearrange his bristles, 'is that Mariana celebrated her eighteenth birthday last year; in March, if I remember correctly.' Receiving nothing other than a blank stare from the girl in the way of confirmation, he forged onwards. 'Under the laws of the Commonwealth, Miss Harris is now of an age to be considered fully and independently responsible for her actions—and, of course, any criminal consequences thereof.'

A stunned silence settled over the table.

'But surely,' ventured Mrs Harris, at last, 'you don't think that our Ana had a hand in any of this horror?'

'To be perfectly frank—which is a greater courtesy than you have shown me,' said Parkes, with a pointed look at the man of the house, 'I don't think that your daughter is in any way responsible for whatever happened to that poor fellow. But,' he held up a peremptory palm as the girl's mother threatened to sink to the ground in sheer relief, 'I'm afraid I must ask her to accompany me to Geraldton, regardless. She's seen the man's face and can help us to produce a sketch of his likeness, at the very least.'

Both husband and wife burst into indistinct, sputtering spiels of shock.

'Really, you can't expect her ...'

'... barely more than a child ...'

'... never been further than Mingenew ...'

'... and the shearing about to start ...'

This time, the protests were cut short by Mariana herself. She pushed back her chair and stood, both palms flat on the table.

'I'll do it,' she said. There was a curious tightness to her mouth, an enigmatic cast to her eyes. 'I shall go—but only if he comes, too.'

The rest of the room turned, following her line of sight to the nameless little friar, who had been so silent throughout the exchange that the Harrises had quite forgotten him. The mendicant himself showed not the slightest sign of surprise at being asked to accompany Mariana, merely signalling his assent with a smile.

'Oh, he's coming,' the detective sergeant said firmly. 'He's wrapped up in this business, and I shan't let him out of my sight till I find out how.'

'Well, that's settled, then,' said the young woman, forcing a false confidence into the phrase. 'I suppose I'd better pack a few things.'

With that, she turned lightly on her heel and strode from

the room, eyes fixed ahead of her as if to look back for only a moment would be to lose her nerve.

The decision, however, had been made. She was going to the coast.

CHAPTER FIVE

It was only the third time that Ana had ridden in a motor car. If she was in any way excited, though, she was doing a thoroughly good job of concealing the fact.

She sat perfectly still—not sullen, but cultivating such a refined air of silent contemplation that it would seem boorish and uncouth to disturb her, even to point out the miraculous patches of wildflowers that sprang from the roadside here and there, or the distant, dusty undulations that sketched the progress of the near-dry Greenough River. The friar sat beside her, equally silent, but the two men in the front were making more than enough noise for the whole party.

Before being sent to fetch the vehicle, Cooper had interviewed the household staff, roustabouts and hired hands, and was currently regaling his superior with a summary of events. The engine of the automobile—a hand-cranked 1913 Ford Tourer which the Perth constabulary had graciously bequeathed to their counterparts in Geraldton after having deemed it to have done its dash—produced such a racket that the tracker was obliged to shout, imbuing his report with a raw urgency thoroughly unjustified by the contents.

'None of them saw a thing, boss!' he bellowed.

'Who did you speak to?' Parkes yelled back.

'Daisy—that's the housemaid—and three young blokes down from Meekatharra.'

'Your lot, or ours?'

The tracker's brow wrinkled in confusion.

'Are they natives?' clarified Parkes.

This time, Cooper nodded. 'They all bunk together in the shed by the stables. Except for Daisy,' he qualified, still at full volume. 'She's got a little room beside the pantry.'

He went on to explain that none of his interviewees had been able to shed much light on the nocturnal happenings of the household. Daisy's little enclave had no windows to the outside and she claimed to have heard nothing in the way of movement after midnight. The lads had spent most of the evening yarning around a small fire by the back paddock, sharing stories and a well-travelled bottle of rum before retiring relatively early. Cooper had inspected both the firepit and the ersatz dormitory; they lay north-east of the house, while Mariana's bedroom window faced west. If she had described her egress with any sort of accuracy, it was entirely in keeping with the assumed order of events that the farmhands would have neither seen nor heard her.

'Any mention of others lurking about?' Parkes shouted.

'The roustabouts reckon there's a fair bit of coming and going at Halfwell; more than the householders are aware of, anyways.'

The detective sergeant nodded. It was part of the natural way of things for rural labourers across the continent. Work was seasonal, sporadic and subject to sudden change; finding a job was often more a question of chance and timing than skill and it was not at all uncommon for men to simply turn up at a station on horseback and try their luck. Of course, with such vast distances separating one prospective employer from the next, being turned away was a significant setback, and those in search of work quickly developed a knack for sniffing out the existing labourers as a point of first contact. Camaraderie and an emerging code of honour furnished newcomers with a bite to eat and a bit of shelter—possibly even a word of introduction to the boss for the particularly fortunate. A few such hopefuls had passed through Halfwell Station in the preceding week, as it happened, but the last had left more than two full days before the brief appearance of the corpse. Still, Cooper had taken down the roustabouts' descriptions of the stranger, just to be sure. Holding the juddering steering wheel on course with one hand, he dug the neatly folded notes from his breast pocket and passed them to his superior. Parkes skimmed the tracker's meticulous lettering as the road swung slowly round to run due south.

The wind thrilled across the vehicle's canvas canopy, adding a cacophonous flutter to the din of the engine and finally rendering all conversation impossible.

Even if the passengers had been able to talk, they would almost certainly have fallen silent at this point, as the rushing plains had thrown up something new and utterly alien. Stunted columns of red dirt struggled towards the sky, looking for all the world like the ruins of some Hittite city ground down by time and age. Parkes twisted in his seat to face the civilians.

'Termite mounds,' he moustached—the sheer scope of his facial foliage rendered him incapable of simply mouthing.

Mariana and the mendicant each struggled to muster an ingratiating expression. The sum of their efforts fell just short of one genuine smile, and both faces faded the very moment Parkes turned his back once more. While the termite towers were a truly exceptional sight, the couple in the back seat were acutely aware of the awkward space they currently occupied: not quite in custody, but far from free. The detective sergeant's intermittent attempts at lightening the mood served only as an uncomfortable reminder of his power over the near-captives. Still, the friar watched the earthen turrets speed by with a flutter of genuine fascination, while Ana—no stranger to her surroundings—lapsed back into solemn silence. It was only when the feats of insect engineering began to be interspersed with works of human construction—silos, sheds and signs—that the young woman began to truly stir, moved by the imminence of Mullewa.

Mullewa was not a big town. At the height of its prosperity, when the prospect of gold lurking beneath the dirt had made a minor miracle of the whole Murchison region, it had still been dwarfed by the more consistent yields to be found at Mount Magnet and Kalgoorlie. Now, less than fifty years after its founding, the dust had settled once more, this time over grain in lieu of gold. Mullewa had gradually eased into its new role as an agricultural centre, providing Geraldton with oats and wheat. As far as Parkes was concerned, there was little more to recommend the place; he considered it a minor outcrop of civilisation, a geographical footnote perched on a potholed dirt road on the way to somewhere more suitable.

For Ana, though, it was a veritable metropolis: it was, simply put, the largest human settlement she had ever seen. From childhood, she had helped her adoptive parents to work the stubborn land. At Halfwell Station, no pair of hands was dispensable and Ana had been kept busy her whole life. The work began with the simple and the safe—mending clothing, helping to keep the house clean—and grew as she did, progressing swiftly to saddling, seeding and other such mainstays of the agrarian experience.

Her mother taught her everything she was able to, while her father had taken the rather ambivalent stance of requiring her assistance in all manner of fieldwork whilst periodically reprimanding her for unfeminine conduct. The whole situation would have been much more satisfactory, Neville Harris would often mutter, if his daughter had simply had the foresight to be born a boy. At these times, Ana had to stifle the urge to respond that, as someone who had made the choice to adopt a child, Neville himself would have been uniquely placed to acquire a male heir, if such a thing had truly been deemed necessary. These impulses had never made the transition to spoken communication, however, as Ana had long ago learned to forgo any allusion to the pre-Harris era of her infancy—the result was an invariable air of sorrow and solemnity, heavy silence or a swift subject-change. Her biological parents, it seemed, had been very close with the Harrises, though they never spoke about them. The little she had managed to discover about her mother and father came from overheard snatches of somnolent sitting-room talk and household gossip.

This dearth of information was something of a rarity, as in all other subjects, Ana was considered rather knowledgeable; she was naturally inquisitive, and there were very few mysteries she failed to solve after having made up her mind to do so. Whatever she couldn't glean from her mother's books or wheedle from itinerant stockmen would be carefully recorded in a small copybook kept beneath Ana's bed. This little ledger would accompany her on the rare occasions when she made it into Mullewa to take communion, after which she was always given an hour or so to rummage through the Sunday-school library.

It was the memory of these blissful, illuminative excursions that caused the girl's heart to quicken as the railway crossing rattled beneath them and the main street came into view. Her current situation in the back seat of a police car notwithstanding, this was as close to freedom as she'd felt for weeks. It wouldn't be entirely fair to say that she felt stifled or stunted at Halfwell. When all was said and done, Ana loved the land she had been raised on, and harboured genuine affection for her adoptive parents. No, the wild, rising freedom she felt as the tin roofs of Mullewa crept into view was not so much a flight from Cinderella serfdom as a compulsion to seek all the beauty and the terror that the wide, impossible world had to offer, hitherto glimpsed only through the words of others: the sprawling cities she knew from Dickens and Dumas; the wide seas traversed by Verne; the gentle, rolling greens of Austen and the rugged outback pastures of Paterson. On the farm, she was an archaeologist, piecing the world together through prose, but a town—small though it might be—provided her with more substantial artefacts. Face pressed to the window, she watched them sweep past—advertisements for motor oil outside the petrol station, packages of exotic food piled high in tin towers beside the general store, even a sign promising the imminent arrival of the travelling picture show, complete with a stencilled likeness of Charlie Chaplin.

Almost imperceptibly, Ana let the stubborn set of her brow soften. As the car slowed and turned into the high street, the fear and trepidation of the last forty-eight hours were once more eclipsed by her customary curiosity and she found herself itching to explore.

With an audible effort, Cooper hauled the steering wheel about and brought the car to a shuddering halt. The town's central street stretched out ahead, a beaten red-dirt ribbon lined with low, tin-roofed buildings. On the northern side crouched the post office, a wood-and-weatherboard assemblage whose telephone connection to Geraldton, first completed some four years earlier, was the talk of the town in a very literal sense. Beyond it, Ana could see the Railway Hotel, its roof sloping at a comfortable angle as if nodding across the street to its namesake.

The station itself was set back from the road in a small oasis of pepper trees and eucalypts—an almost garish display of greenery against the sparse expanse beyond, seeming to hint at the distant landscapes that could be found if one were to follow the tracks.

'Come on, then.' Parkes heaved himself out of the vehicle and landed with a dust-raising thud. He stretched for a moment, blinking, before trudging round to open the back door and usher his charges through the heat of the day to the relative respite of the post office.

The mendicant paused before the door, his attention captured by the unmistakeable outline of a cathedral spire in the middle distance. It was only a glimpse, the upper extremity peeking out from the surrounding rooftops, but it was enough to make him test his tenuous freedom. He turned, preparing to petition his captor, but Parkes cut him off with a single stony shake of the head.

One by one, the party shuffled through the post office door, with the exception of Cooper, who peeled off to pursue his own errands. As a general rule, white townspeople had little time for the area's original inhabitants and would make their disapproval known in any way possible. The presence of Parkes would protect Cooper from outright abuse (as long as his skills continued to prove useful) but loaded looks and casual deprecation were enough for him to seek the friendlier faces awaiting him on the outskirts of town.

Inside the post office, a single electric bulb struggled to shed light on shelves piled with stamps, stationery and all manner of papers and periodicals in varying stages of obsolescence. A low counter stretched the length of the northern wall, staffed by a smiling young woman in a heavily starched blouse of vaguely official cut. A small wooden sign on the counter identified her as 'Elizabeth Williams, Postmistress', though she could be more completely described as the town's telegraph operator, stationer, newsagent, stenographer, purveyor of rumour, semi-official pianist, and occasional correspondent to the *Geraldton Guardian* on matters of local interest, including subjects as far-ranging as births, deaths, marriages, sporting fixtures and the ever-enthralling bi-monthly meetings of the Mullewa Road Board.

'Mariana Harris!' she cried. 'You're a sight as rare as the rains! Must be three years since you were last in town. And—why, is that Arnold Parkes? My word! Whatever brings you all the way out here? Nothing serious, I hope?'

'Missing person, I'm afraid,' replied Parkes, gravely. 'I'll need you to send a description round to every office in the area.'

While Elizabeth reached for her carbon paper, Parkes turned to Ana.

'Don't leave out a single detail,' he instructed. 'You're the only one to have actually seen this chap so you must be as thorough as you possibly can.'

'I'll try, though I truly couldn't see much in the dark.' She hesitated, hands wandering towards her locket. 'I've never dictated a telegram before. Will I need to say "stop", and all the rest of it?'

Miss Williams laughed. 'Leave all of that to me. All you need to do is tell me what you saw. There's every chance that I shall be able to tell you who the poor fellow is, and there'll be no need to send a telegram at all. After all, I know just about every soul within fifty miles of this desk. Here's a rare thing, though— I can't say I've had the pleasure of meeting your companion.' Shrewd and clever above the careful warmth of her smile, her eyes skipped to the little friar, taking him in, from crude cassock to roughened sandals. Having all-too-recently undergone the lengthy process of introducing someone with no name, however, Parkes felt compelled to intervene.

'As much as I regret having to curtail the formalities,' he said, moustache crinkling, 'time is at something of a premium. If the man isn't dead already, he'll be devilish close before we're done here.'

'Of course.' Miss Williams shook herself straight and motioned Ana to a seat. 'Best we get started, then. What did he look like?'

Ana ran through the same basic description of the missing man that she had given Parkes—tall, thin, pale and bearded— fleshing it out with such stray observations and points of detail as she could call to mind. The man had been neither notably young nor particularly old, Ana only being able to place him somewhere between the respective ages of herself and Detective Sergeant Parkes, an interval of some thirty-five years. His eyes had been lidded, so she could hazard no guess as to their colour, and in any case, moonlight had meddled considerably with the palette of her perception.

'Anything else?' asked Miss Williams, raising her voice above the scratchy flurry of shorthand.

Ana hesitated, thinking.

'Freckles,' she said, softly. Then with more conviction: '*Si, claro*, he was freckled, and he wore rather a lot of clothing. Heavy fabrics; an undershirt and a long coat.'

The pencil paused.

'Is that out of the ordinary?' Miss Williams enquired.

'At this time of year, it is. Most of the stockmen we get through the station roll up their sleeves and pack their coats away. The night's hot enough as it is.'

'I see. Did he have a hat?'

'Not that I noticed, though it may have been knocked clear as he fell.'

Miss Williams wrote in silence for a few moments more. Then, clearing her throat, she read the full description aloud, her sharp diction filling every corner of the gloomy office. With a solemn nod, Ana acknowledged it as an accurate enough picture of the man she had left on the dark sand.

'What do you think, Lizzie?' asked Parkes of the postmistress. 'Can you put a name to him?'

'It's rather hard to say,' she sighed. 'Any number of swagmen could fit that description, to a greater or lesser extent. Then there are all the others who pass through—prospectors, salesmen, all manner of surveyors and other government types.'

Parkes shook his head, moustache swaying. 'Hasn't given us much to work with, has he? Surely the decent thing to do, if one planned to go missing, would be to fit oneself out with some sort of distinguishing mark—an eye patch, or a scar at the very least. Isn't that right, Ana?'

Seeing that Parkes would not proceed with his wit unapplauded, Ana winched her lip into the barest semblance of a smile. Satisfied, the officer turned back to the desk.

'Well, the poor bloke was heading this way—he must have been bound for Mullewa. Who's due through town this month?'

Miss Williams considered. 'Well, the picture show will be here next week; I suppose young Chudleigh, the projectionist, could fit the bill. He's certainly tall enough, and he often lets his whiskers grow long—probably hoping to hide that weak chin of his, poor lad. Then, too, there's Beynon, the electric fellow; he'll be due through anytime this week. I suppose he could fit the description easily enough.'

The detective sergeant nodded, scribbling in his notebook. The names were familiar to him, though he had no faces to hang them on.

'The only other fellow who springs to mind,' the postmistress went on, 'would be Jack Rollins, who comes back down from Carnarvon now and then to help his uncle out with the harvest.'

Parkes sighed, rapping distractedly on the desk. 'Not much, I suppose, but it'll do for a start. Jot their names down, there's a good girl, and wire them over to Geraldton along with the description. My men'll follow them up at the station.'

Elizabeth Williams obliged, smiling professionally through the condescension.

'Meanwhile,' the detective sergeant went on, 'I'd better pop over and bring the local lads up to speed.' He strode to a dusty window and peered out towards the tin-roofed shed that housed the Mullewa Police Department. 'At any rate, it's getting dark. They'll have to wrap up the search soon enough.' He sighed. 'Nothing more to be done today.'

* * *

Ana's eyes snapped open. She had been dreaming.

Vague nightmare fragments still clung to her hair and caught in the folds of her nightgown. Termites swarmed and massed in the darkness around her, waiting to drag her across the bloodied

54

bush and entomb her in a massive, ruinous monolith, a tower of dirt so high it threatened to blight the moon.

She shook her head, knuckling the sand from her eyes.

A high, white ceiling of beaten tin swam into view, shadows deepening the finely embossed flowers. For a long moment, Ana struggled to place it. Gradually, as her eyes adjusted to the dim, diffuse starlight seeping in at the corners of the curtains, the rest of the room crept into view. Beyond the stiff, white bedsheets stretched taut between her toes, a sullen wardrobe hulked against faded floral wallpaper. A walnut duchess dressing table crouched in the far corner, the coiled chain of Ana's locket glinting dimly atop it. Recollection came suddenly: she was in the Railway Hotel.

A moment later, the sound that had shaken her from sleep repeated itself—three short, sharp taps from the other side of the door. Ana drew her knees to her chest, making a stiff marquee of the bedclothes.

She waited. Sweltering silence crept past—ten seconds, twenty seconds—before the tapping sounded again. It was neither hurried nor insistent; Ana could almost have mistaken it for the building settling or the percussive pressure of distant pipes, were it not for the way the doorknob shook with each gentle tap, the cool ceramic twitching visibly in the moonlight.

Slowly, carefully, she drew the covers back. She lowered first one foot, then the other, wincing at the creaks her stockinged weight wrung from the floor. Inching her way across the cool jarrah, she rolled the too-long sleeves of her nightgown with tingling fingers. The doorknob was cold to the touch; she gripped it, and the tapping stopped. So, too, did her breath. For a long moment, the silence was absolute. Then, before her courage had time enough to fail, Ana wrenched the door open.

There, half-shadowed in the dim hallway, was the mendicant. 'I've been thinking,' he said.

Any relief that Ana had felt at sighting a familiar face

evaporated as she met the man's eyes; his customary smile was nowhere to be found.

'Last night,' he said, 'you took me to see a body.'

He spoke quickly, but his tone was matter-of-fact, mercifully devoid of malice or judgement.

'You expected a body, in fact, but found none.'

Ana said nothing.

'Why should that be such a shock?' the friar wondered. 'With a little imagination, any number of possible explanations emerge. The poor man might, for example, simply have been stunned; he could've recovered his wits enough after a few hours to stumble onwards. Then again, he might just as easily have been found by a passing swagman, hauled up on horseback and carried back to safety. There was even the possibility, of course, that the would-be murderer had returned, waiting only long enough to make sure you had gone before bringing his grisly task to completion. Not one of these scenarios occurred to you, though. Why should that be?'

Unwilling to wait, the mendicant obliged himself with the answer.

'Because you *knew*, of course,' he said. 'You knew quite well that the fellow was dead. You had crept back to check on him before coming to confide in me. You said it yourself, in that first sting of shock—you said the body had been there *just a moment ago*, though I was too distracted at the time to pay it any heed.'

Ana held her silence, but the effort it cost her was plain to see. It was written in the fitful shadows that played over her lips and the force with which her bloodless fingers gripped the doorjamb.

The friar sighed. 'Then comes the hardest question,' he said, softer now. 'What could cause you to omit such a pertinent piece of information from your statement? Not guilt, surely; after all, if you had somehow hastened our mystery man to his demise, why tell the story at all? In my experience, a sinner will confess completely, or not at all.'

'You think I'm innocent, then?'

The words were muddy with sleep and hope. Ana winced to hear the childish hope in her own voice, sounding foolish and small in the darkness.

'Innocent?' The mendicant let slip the hint of a smile. 'I couldn't very well say that. In fact, my vocation rather relies on the opposite; the predication that none of us is truly innocent is rather the nature of the game, I'm afraid.' Seeing that his words did little to comfort the girl, he hurried onwards. 'I do remain convinced, however, that you had no hand in the man's death.'

Several seconds passed in the musty silence of the hotel hallway.

'I didn't mean to lie,' Ana said, at last. 'I could see the suspicion in the detective sergeant's eyes—I suppose that's what his vocation relies on, isn't it? Suspicion?—and I just wanted to ... oh, I don't know!' This last expostulation was accompanied with a queer sort of shiver. 'Why did you never ask me what really happened? Why don't you ask me now?'

'If I asked you now, would you tell me the truth?' Seeing the answer in the girl's eyes, he went on. 'No. There's a reason you didn't tell me what happened that night and there's a reason you won't tell me now. I won't ask you to give it—not until you're ready—but I do have some advice for you: the truth will not be hidden forever.'

The mendicant seemed to age under the weight of his words. His voice sank.

'Trust me,' he said. 'In this, if in nothing else, I know whereof I speak. The truth will not be hidden forever. If you do not seek it, it will seek you. It will follow you over land and sea. It will devastate; it will lay you to waste.' His eyes met Ana's. 'The life you build from the rubble, though—well, what you make of it is up to you.'

Abruptly, he turned to go. It was several moments before Ana had recovered her reason enough to call after him.

'Wait!' she hissed into the dark. 'Are you going to tell him? Are you going to tell Parkes?'

The mendicant paused at the edge of the stairwell, almost entirely swallowed by shadow, and looked back over his shoulder.

'No,' he said, simply. 'You will—when the time is right.'

With that, he melted into the darkness. Aside from a window swinging open at the end of the hall, all was still.

CHAPTER SIX

Breakfast was a strained affair.

Detective Sergeant Parkes sat stiffly behind his full English, heaping beans over a forkful of sausage and glaring across the table. The object of his ire was the mendicant, who was himself cheerfully engaged in the twofold task of eviscerating a large orange and completely ignoring Parkes. Equidistant between the pair, in terms of mood, geography and appetite, sat Mariana, busy making her way through a thick slice of toast topped liberally with marmalade.

A certain scent hung heavy on the dining room—the cumulative effect of years of stale beer and cigarette smoke. A strict ban on smoking at the breakfast table had been introduced but no such prohibition was in place for lunch or dinner, which, due to the constraints incumbent on a small-town hotel, were served at the same table. The November sun seeping in through the windows did little to alleviate the tension, bringing with it a heat far too advanced for the hour.

At root, however, the conflict was more than merely environmental: it had its origins in the early hours of the same morning, when the mendicant had returned to the room he was sharing with Detective Sergeant Parkes. The door's aging oak opened only with the strongest encouragement and the resultant sound—a species of drawn-out, shuddering creak—had jolted Parkes from a rather pleasant dream in which he was halfway through shaving his moustache, causing him to awaken with an altogether undignified shriek. Not having reached his age and stage without learning a thing or two, however, the resolute lawman was able to swiftly transform his yell into an accusation. Could the friar deny, after all, that he had been sneaking about the hallways after dark? Was there any clearer sign of guilt than creeping away in the middle of the night and trying to effect an escape?

The detective sergeant's embarrassment was completed by the friar's calm counterpoint—namely, that escapes are usually effected by leaving a room, as opposed to entering—and the simmering resentment thus produced had kept the officer awake for the remainder of the night.

Despite not being privy to any of these nocturnal goings-on, Ana knew immediately upon entering the dining room that something was amiss. Judging quite rightly that this particular breakfast was not the time to come out with a confession, she opted instead to finish her toast in silence. Sooner or later, she hoped, an opportunity would present itself.

As if in answer to her unspoken appeal, the door to the dining room swung open and one of the hotel staff approached. The lad revealed—in somewhat hushed tones, as if divulging a secret—that 'a coloured gentleman' was waiting outside for the detective sergeant.

A quick look made its way around the table. They were not due to meet Cooper at the police station for nearly two hours; if he had come early, it was surely to bring news. In a moment, the early-morning enmities were forgotten, left to cool alongside the detective sergeant's abandoned beans as the party made its way outside.

Cooper was waiting for them beside the Ford, his lean limbs artfully arranged to fit within the sparse shade it afforded.

'They found a body,' he said, wasting no time on formalities.

A ripple ran through his audience.

'Where?' the three demanded, in imperfect unison.

'Just past Wongoondy. About halfway to Mingenew,' Cooper elaborated, in response to the blank faces of Ana and the friar.

'But that's ridiculous,' said Parkes, pulling at his moustache. 'Why, there's nothing at all between here and Mingenew. Where was he found, exactly? Who called it in?'

For the first time, Cooper looked uncomfortable. He cast a quick look at Ana; possibly the first time the deferential tracker had done so, she reflected. It was certainly the first time she had noticed the fine flecks of green in his earthy eyes, the depth of compassion they contained. Compassion, and something else, too. Before she could fully explore it, though, the look was gone. The tracker coughed.

'Might not be the best place to discuss it, boss,' he said, nodding in Ana's direction. 'Bit graphic, if you understand.'

Ana bristled, her warm feelings lost in the flushing heat of indignation. 'If you're afraid I'll swoon at the mention of blood, Mr Cooper, you can go ahead and lay those fears to rest. I didn't faint delivering my first lamb, I've consistently kept my head whilst depriving chooks of theirs, and when I saw that man attacked—terrible though it was—I lived to tell the tale. In fact,' she went on, rolling up the heavy sleeves of her dress, 'the only thing that poses any real danger of making me swoon, at present, is the sun, so you'd do well to spill your story as swiftly as possible.'

The friar laughed his raucous approval, and even Parkes had to hide a smile—it was impossible not to, seeing Cooper's usually impassive face transformed so thoroughly by this spirited rebuke.

'You can tell us on the road, Cooper,' said Parkes, pulling the driver's-side door open. 'If Miss Harris does faint, at least she'll be sitting down.'

* * *

Though early, the heat of the day had already managed to make an oven of the vehicle's interior. The leather seats seemed almost on the point of smoking and the dark steel of the driving instruments could be handled only with the aid of an intermediary material (when gloves proved insufficient, Parkes folded his handkerchief several times over the wheel). An aging suspension system compounded the passengers' discomfort. Every rut, rock and pothole made itself fully felt, and the railway crossing was rough enough to lift the little friar fully three inches from his seat. Despite these trials, however, complaints were few and far between—the collective attention was focussed far too fully on the narrative of the corpse's recovery.

The man in question—if he was, indeed, the same unfortunate fellow who had fallen beside Ana three nights earlier—appeared to have made quite a journey. His body had been recovered from a pigsty on one of the stations near Wongoondy, some twenty miles south of Mullewa. Whether he was alive on entering the enclosure could not be ascertained but the simple fact of his death was now no longer in dispute. With characteristically indiscriminate appetites, the pigs had managed to deprive the poor fellow of nearly a third of his body.

'That'll be why he was thrown to the pigs,' said Parkes. 'They'll eat anything and everything, the brutes—no better way to dispose of the evidence. If there was ever any doubt about this being a deliberate act of murder, I'd say the question is now well and truly settled.'

'It certainly can't have been a suicide,' the friar agreed, in rare concord with the policeman. Having taken more confessions than he cared to count—and counselling many a soul away from contemplating that most ungrateful affront to the divine—he felt qualified to impart an opinion. 'I should think that even the most thoroughly guilt-ridden wretch would shy away from consigning himself to a pig pit.'

As one, they all fell silent, contemplating the poor man's hideous end.

'The plan didn't work, though, did it?' observed Ana, at last. 'Most of the body is still there.'

'Don't think the murderer knew much about raising pigs,' said Cooper. 'Must've heaved the body over in the middle of the night, thinking it'd be gone by the morning. In this heat, though, they feed 'em their slops after sunset—the pigs're too lazy to eat, otherwise. They would've been too full to do the body much damage.'

In spite of her earlier assertions, Ana couldn't help feeling a little queasy in considering these details.

'Did the message say what was left?' asked Parkes. Reasoning that speed was of the essence, they had not wasted any time in visiting Miss Williams to go over the telegrams a second time. Cooper had heard it all, and an uncommonly strong memory was one of the faculties which made him so useful to the constabulary.

'Face is all but gone,' he said, grimly. 'Photographer's not gunna be any use—they're sending someone out to make a sketch. Boss in Geraldton reckons that's the only way to get an idea of how the bloke looked.'

Parkes gave a start, his grip on the wheel noticeably tightening.

'What? Who are they sending?' he demanded.

'Dawson. Should be on the train now, I reckon.'

'*Dawson*?' The detective sergeant forgot himself enough to swear.

'A friend of yours?' the friar enquired, rather antagonistic in his enjoyment. Parkes, however, refused to be drawn, sinking instead into sullen silence. The conversation carried on without him for a time but his subdued mood soon settled over the rest of the vehicle, and before long, each of the passengers was left to their thoughts.

Ana gazed out through the dust-rimmed window, watching the world flicker past. Despite the grisly reality which awaited her—or perhaps because of it—her mind flitted over simple, childish concerns. Chief amongst them was the churlish disappointment of being cheated out of a trip to Geraldton. She had never been to the coast, or indeed seen a larger body of water than the miserly Mullewa Creek. To Ana, the ocean was a huge, heaving mystery, something glimpsed only through stories and song. The three simple seashells her mother kept on the mantle were as precious and alien to her as relics recovered from ancient Babylonia, and she had spent so many hours turning them over in her hands that the fragile little things had long ago been polished smooth. Sometimes, she would hold them to her ear to hear the voice of the sea, fancying that she could divine some secret truth from its sibilance; at other times, she would simply sit and hold them, meditating on the ocean's impossible magnitude.

Despite these lengthy reflections, she had never fully been able to reconcile herself to the idea that a sailor could step on board a vessel in Sydney and be carried all the way to Madagascar, or Manchester—or to Chile.

It amazed her that at this very moment, the waters lapping on the shore at Geraldton were essentially inseparable from the waves that broke upon the sands of Santiago, in her father's native land. He had taken a single step, boarded a simple boat, and that vast expanse—large enough to swallow the very curvature of the earth—had cradled him, kept him safe, carried him halfway around the world. And then what? Ana couldn't say. As always, she had to remind herself that she knew next to nothing of her father, and less still of her mother. She shook the thoughts clear of her head. How had she ended up at that old, weathered query? She cast about for something to distract herself and realised that the car was no longer moving.

CHAPTER SEVEN

The property near Wongoondy was smaller than Halfwell Station.

The house itself was a squat, simple thing of tin and timber, surrounded by withered trees and a collection of small sheds to which particulars of the domestic process had been delegated. A rusted wringer bolted to the side of one structure marked it as a laundry, while another lean-to seemed to serve as a kitchen. Further out, past the outhouse and the stables, lay the current locus of activity: a ramshackle, vaguely circular enclosure in the meagre shade of a few ghost gums.

Even from a distance, the pigsty's olfactory presence was oppressive, and the scent only grew more powerful as the party approached. Several people were already gathered around the enclosure. Ana felt quite confident in assuming that the eldest of those attendant—a tall, lean man with a dog at his heels—was the farm's proprietor. The two men closest to him, both peering uncomfortably over the edge of the enclosure, might be sons or associates, while the weathered-looking fellow propped against the fence had the air of a swagman. There was a lady present, too, though the way her gaze roamed brazenly across the terrible scene in the pigsty was anything but ladylike. The farmer's wife, it seemed to Ana; she had probably seen more than her fair share of birth, death and everything in between. The final member of the crowd—a young man in the uniform of the Geraldton police—could only be Dawson, though Ana could find nothing in his wide, amiable face to merit the detective sergeant's strange antipathy.

The first of Ana's assumptions was proven sound when the man with the dog stepped forward, introducing himself as one Jack Lucas, a lifetime pastoralist whose long years on the land had hitherto held no interest at all for the members of the constabulary. So eager was he in bringing this point to the detective sergeant's immediate notice, in fact, that Parkes resolved at once to scour the archives for any unsolved cases in the vicinity of Wongoondy.

If Lucas was at all surprised to see the detective sergeant flanked by an indigenous tracker, a bareheaded priest and a young woman in hand-me-downs, he gave no sign. To be fair, though, Ana doubted the extent to which the farmer's sun-fissured face was capable of any expression other than the weary resilience it currently wore; it might as well have been carved out of gnarled olive-wood, for all the movement on display. Through imperceptibly parted lips, he told what little there was to tell.

Yesterday, he assured them, had been a day as devoid of anything that might interest the police as any other day on his property. Fences had been checked, machinery oiled, bores lifted, animals fed and watered. That night, Lucas had been the last to turn in, as was his custom. He had gone to bed just after ten thirty, after banking down the fire in the kitchen and turning off the hallway lamps. His son had retired to his room some hours earlier—the hale lad's rather more strenuous share of the physical labour having worn him out—and the servants and swaggies were already holed up in their shed by the laundry. Lucas was prepared to swear to this last point, as he had a full view of their darkened door from the kitchen window; not a drop of light leaked through the rough-fitted frame.

If the day had been uneventful, the night was positively peaceful.

Not one of the farm's inhabitants reported anything other than a profound sleep; not the slightest snap of a twig shook the silence, which was broken only when the magpies woke to usher in the dawn with their cries. It wasn't until after breakfast, when one of the swaggies was sent to sling the table scraps into the sty and top the pigs' trough up with water, that the body was finally discovered.

The same story, thought Parkes. History repeating itself. Miles from civilisation, no rhyme or reason—just a body. This time, though, the body had not disappeared. The remains, so to speak, remained, in spite of the murderer's best efforts to effect otherwise. On that front, at least, the situation was much simpler.

'Right, then!' barked the detective sergeant, turning to address the small assembly. 'I shall require everyone not immediately essential to proceedings to vacate the area. Poor old Cooper'll have trouble enough making sense of these tracks without the lot of you traipsing back and forth all over the evidence.'

One by one, the onlookers began to peel away towards the homestead. Cooper set off in the opposite direction, treading the dusty tracks with the utmost care, making his way slowly but steadily along a trail discernible only to himself. Into the resultant vacuum stepped the young constable, who had until now been waiting in the wings with a good-natured smile wholly at odds with the grimness of the environs.

'The poor boy seems not to be aware of the detective sergeant's antagonism,' came a whisper at Ana's ear. She turned to see the friar, his eyes creased in concern. She had to nod; there was certainly no outward indication of bad blood between the pair, despite the previous outburst from Parkes. The policemen were now speaking in low, business-like tones, comparing perspectives and checking for chinks in witness accounts. No particularly illuminating titbits leapt out at the eavesdroppers—at least, not until the conversation concluded.

'That's all from my end, sir,' said the constable. He then coughed, hesitating for the first time. 'Will you—will you be wanting to speak to Dawson now?'

Ana and the friar shared a look.

'There's absolutely nothing I want less, my lad,' said the detective sergeant, his moustache wrinkling in distaste, 'but needs must and all that.'

'Come now, Arnold!' a voice rang out. 'Surely I merit the full proverb? You've never before baulked at comparing me to the devil.'

Four pairs of feet swivelled as one, drawing from the sand an impressive sibilance.

At close proximity, it seemed almost ludicrous that Ana could have mistaken the woman now striding past her for Mr Lucas's wife. Where the farmer was stolid and simple, this woman was powered by an almost fierce energy; every movement, down to the slightest set of an eyebrow, was rife with humour, hunger and curiosity. She stopped less than a foot from the detective sergeant's face, folding her arms.

'You will address me by my title,' the police officer seethed, 'as befits your rank.'

'I don't have a rank, Arnold,' she said, 'though you've had chances enough to give me one. I am currently a civilian consultant, here only as a personal favour to my dear old friend Stevie—or Assistant Commissioner Robinson, as you might know him.'

'If you were a man, I'd thump you for that attitude.'

'If you were a man, you'd find the strength to restrain yourself,' responded Dawson, without so much as a pause. 'Now, as enjoyable as it is to run rings around you, darling, I didn't come halfway to the back end of Hades just to watch you strain your wits. I was sent here because there is no-one currently in the employ of the Geraldton constabulary who can do what I do.'

'What do you do?'

Ana was almost shocked to hear the question leave her own mouth. Dawson turned, regarding her for the first time. Cool, grey eyes moved behind modish spectacles as she looked the younger woman up and down.

'I draw pictures, my dear.' She strode forward, holding out a long-fingered hand. 'Madeleine Dawson. Don't call me Maddie, or you shall fare scarcely better than our poor friend over there,' she warned, indicating the pigsty with a delicate movement of her eyebrow. 'And what is it that you do?'

Ana was caught off guard.

'I don't know,' she admitted. In an effort to divert attention, she made a panicked grab at her neighbour's cassock. 'He's a friar.'

'He is indeed,' said Ms Dawson. Without removing her gaze from the mendicant, she raised her voice to address Parkes. 'Uncommonly thoughtful of you, Arnold, to arrange for an officiant, though there's still rather a lot to be done before we're ready for a burial, I'm afraid.'

For a long moment, the only sound was the low, slow grinding of molars from behind the detective sergeant's moustache. Eventually, with a visibly Herculean effort, he managed to wrest aside his injured pride.

'Miss Harris is the witness,' he growled. 'If you'd be so good as to lay aside the posturing and show her your sketch ...'

Madeleine Dawson rewarded her rival by sparing him the sting of her repartee. Without a further word, she beckoned Ana over to the little copse of ghost gums. There, kneeling in the shade, she extracted a leather-bound folio from her pocketbook. The pages turned quickly, loosing tantalising fragments of worlds caught in charcoal. Ana craned her neck to catch a glimpse of a horse's mane, its motion captured in a few matchless strokes of monochrome, a dragonfly reflected, flawless, in the surface of a pond, a clutch of three gum blossoms perfect enough to evoke the forest in its entirety.

So transported was Ana by the beauty of the preceding sketches that she didn't recognise the face until she had been staring at it for several seconds. When the man's features finally registered, it was to the accompaniment of a sharp, sudden breath.

'Is it him?' asked Madeleine, her voice tempered for the first time with a semblance of warmth.

Ana nodded.

'Would you be able to swear to it?'

'I would,' said Ana, still scanning the image with fevered eyes.

In life, she had only seen the man for a moment; barely longer in death. His face then had been contorted, pulled awry by pain and terror. In her sketch, Madeleine had not merely resurrected the man; she had set him to rest. Ana could see now that the man's eyes were large—not, as they had been, in the fright-wide throes of shock, but deep and dark, placid beneath their full lashes. Yes, she knew him. His beard was slightly different, perhaps, his nose a little too long, but the overall resemblance was unmistakeable. A kind face, a face that looked as if it might break into a smile at any moment. Then again, how much could one tell from a sketch, even one as well executed as this? The emperor Caligula's features looked regal enough when set in stone.

'Was it hard?' wondered Ana. 'Drawing this, I mean?'

'It didn't take me long, if that's what you're asking—when you've been sketching as long as I have, it rather becomes second nature.' Madeleine's face tightened. 'The job is far from pleasant, though. If that poor wretch's face had been intact, it would've been enough for the constable to set up his tripod and take a photograph. My services are only called for when the facial damage is severe enough to render the subject wholly unrecognisable.'

Ana shivered. 'How do you do it, then?' she asked. 'How do you know what he looked like?'

'I read the remains,' said Madeleine, distant-eyed. 'There are clues, you know, in the bone and sinew. Just as an architect may study a blueprint and know what the finished building should look like, so too can the flesh be studied.'

'But that's incredible! Where did you learn how to do that?'

'In France.'

Ana's eyes lit up, stoked by the secret, story-fed wanderlust hidden away deep at her core.

'Did you study in Paris?'

'I'm afraid my instruction was rather more Somme than Sorbonne,' said Madeleine, forcing a tight-lipped smile. 'I was with the reserve nursing service. There's nothing quite like war for showing you what lies beneath a man's skin.'

'Oh,' said Ana, casting about for something remotely appropriate to say. 'I see,' she came up with, rather feebly.

'You will soon, I'm afraid,' said Madeleine. 'I doubt very much that a sketch alone would be enough to satisfy our friend the detective sergeant; he is not a great admirer of my work.'

Ana took a moment to process this.

'I shall have to look at him, then?' she said. 'At—at the body?'

'You shall,' intoned Parkes, intruding on the conversation with a suddenness that made both women jump. 'Though it pleases me little to subject a young lady to something so gruesome, there is still a protocol that must be followed in situations such as these.' This last statement was directed for some reason at Madeleine, as if the whole unpleasantness was somehow her doing. 'The sooner this is over and done with, the better.'

'Don't let him rush you,' said Madeleine, ostensibly to Ana, though her gaze was firmly locked with the detective sergeant's. Parkes pulled at his moustache, ready to retort, but before he could muster a suitably scathing response, Ana took her leave.

Chin set, spine straight, she walked directly between the two combatants and out into the sunlight, heading for the pigsty. The little friar hurried from his patch of shade to join her. He was followed some seconds later by Parkes, Madeleine Dawson and the young constable, who had been nodding off in the shade of the water tank and was now eager to be seen to be doing something.

The little crowd clustered around Ana in an uncomfortable semicircle, distant enough to be decorous, but close enough to sate the collective curiosity born of death, dust and boredom.

For a moment, there was silence. Ana had stopped about six feet from the fence, eyes fixed on the horizon. Sensing her hesitation, the mendicant stepped forward to offer his hand. Ana looked at it as if seeing a human limb for the first time, then dismissed it with a small smile. Alone, she took one step forward, then another, then another.

Suddenly, she was there.

She stared down into the muck, gripping the fence post so hard that tiny splinters began to work their way into her hands. She paid them no heed. Every last ounce of energy she possessed was occupied in keeping her body still and standing. She would not scream, she would not fall, she would not look away. Her jaw was clamped shut. She dared not open it, not even to take a breath, afraid of what might escape if she did so. Only when the need to breathe became too great did she finally look away, her step faltering slightly as she turned.

'Is it him?' asked Parkes, hastening to take her arm. She shrugged him off.

'I don't know,' she said. She drew a deep, shuddering breath. 'How could I? His face is a ruin! There's hardly any hair left—not a scrap of clothing ...'

'Does it look like him, though?' Parkes demanded. 'The height, the colouring?'

The question hung for a moment. Ana fidgeted with the silver chain of her locket.

'It does,' she said at last.

'Did you say there was no clothing?' This next query came

not from the policeman, but the friar. Without waiting for an answer, he moved to the fence and looked over. 'None,' he muttered. 'None at all.'

'Is this a worthwhile observation?' snapped Parkes; the friar's interest struck him as verging on the indecent.

'No,' said Ana, holding up a hand. 'He's right! Not so much as a tatter of cloth.'

'Pigs'll eat anything,' said Parkes. 'I think that's been well established.'

The mendicant nodded. 'Insatiable beasts,' he agreed. 'But look—they haven't turned him over. He was dumped in there on his back, and the flesh has only been eaten from the front.'

Parkes wrinkled his moustache in distaste, either unwilling or unable to follow the current line of reasoning.

'If the man had been wearing any clothing,' explained Ana, impatiently, 'we'd still be able to see some of it—it'd be beneath him.'

'The murderer undressed him, of course,' said Parkes, as if the idea had occurred to him immediately. 'It makes sense, you see. Makes it easier for the pigs to get at him.'

'The murderer would then have to find another way to rid himself of the clothing,' said the friar. He paused a moment in thought. 'Perhaps the shirt bore an insignia of some sort; a distinguishing feature. Perhaps he wasn't concerned with disposing of the body so much as ensuring that it could not be identified—hence the pigs.'

This possibility had not occurred to the detective sergeant, and he was less than thrilled to have it brought to his attention by an amateur.

'Perhaps,' he said, 'you should do your own job instead of trying to do mine. It's a little late for last rites, but I'm sure a prayer or two would not go amiss.' He turned. 'And you, Miss Harris, had better go and write to your parents. They'll need to be apprised of the latest developments.'

Ana hesitated, casting a look at the mendicant. The little man opened his mouth to protest but seemed to think better of it. He sighed.

Reaching into his cassock, he pulled out a rough wooden rosary, the beads clinking hollowly against one another as he returned to the fence. The others backed away in respectful discomfort as he bowed his head and began softly to chant.

CHAPTER EIGHT

The sun had sunk below the horizon, but the hot, dull heat of the afternoon gave no indication of abating. Ana reclined on a tired wicker couch on the back verandah, engaged in an activity that, to the uninformed observer, almost resembled reading.

Madeleine Dawson, however, was far from uninformed.

'You've been staring at the same sentence for fifteen minutes, darling. Either it's a bore of a book, or you've something else on your mind entirely.'

Ana sighed. 'It's just a lot to take in,' she said.

The vague wave of the hand with which she accompanied this statement was clearly intended to encompass the events of the preceding three days in their entirety. A few hours earlier, Cooper had returned with news of the murderer's trail: a single two-wheeled trap heading south. What was more, the tracker informed them, the distance between hoof prints diminished noticeably over the miles. The horse was tiring.

The effect of these tidings on Detective Sergeant Parkes had been rather extraordinary: for the first time in days, he was on familiar ground. Furnished at last with a trail, a fugitive, and something in the way of evidence, he flung open the door of the Ford and fairly leapt into the driver's seat, barking instructions as Cooper cranked the engine. Moments later, they were gone.

The dust kicked up by their departure floated about for a few desultory minutes before settling on a new and rather uncomfortable state of affairs. As per the detective sergeant's decree—heard only dimly over the din of the engine and received little better—Ana and the friar remained in remand. Their new custodian was the constable, who had finally been introduced as William Johns of the Geraldton police. He proved to be an amiable enough young man, if somewhat unprepared for the burden of command. The situation of which he now found himself ostensibly in charge was more than a little strained.

Upon leaving the police station that morning, his instructions had been simple. He was to accompany Miss Dawson out to the Tardun siding on the train, and then see her safely past Wongoondy to the scene of the crime. This had been accomplished easily enough. The train journey was uneventful, and they had managed to cadge a lift from the railway siding with one of Lucas's station hands. The subsequent return to Geraldton had not been given a great deal of thought, it having simply been assumed that the detective sergeant would conduct his various charges homewards via motor car. With the vehicle now gone, Constable Johns supposed that the next best option would be to return to the coast via railway.

He was soon to discover, however, that the 'daily service' operating on the section of the Murchison line in question had perhaps been advertised a little too literally: the train really did run only once per day, obliging those who sought a return journey to wait a full twenty-four hours. Constable Johns now found himself in the thoroughly unenviable position of having to prevail upon old Lucas for a night's hospitality. It was no small favour to ask—the peculiar pair now in his custody would also require accommodation, of course, to say nothing of Ms Dawson, who was less than enthusiastic about having her artistic services repaid with a night of rural detention.

Perhaps the most reluctant party to the proposition, though, was the landowner himself.

He had been leery of having law enforcement on his property

from the beginning, and the addition of a beggar-monk and a couple of stray women did little to sweeten the deal. In the end, however, thinly veiled threats of a legally punitive nature won out where appeals to kindness and civic duty had failed. When the possibility of a weekly police patrol through Wongoondy was raised, Mr Lucas went so far as to offer up his own room for the use of his esteemed lady guests. This being politely declined, it was eventually agreed that Ana and Ms Dawson would take the sitting room for the night. Constable Johns was given a bed in the room by the kitchen. Its usual occupant, one of the station hands, was relegated for the time being to a dusty lean-to amongst the outbuildings. After swearing solemnly on the good book to make no attempts at escape, the friar was permitted to string his old hammock across the verandah.

With everyone suitably accommodated, a subdued supper was taken in the dining room. Mr Lucas proposed a nightcap— having remembered the bottle of fine Irish whiskey in his pantry after a chance remark from Constable Johns on the subject of hitherto-unsolved thefts from a neighbouring farm—and all those present responded with considerably more enthusiasm than had been on display throughout the evening thus far. It was at this point that Ana, Madeleine and the mendicant had excused themselves and moved outside.

On the partially enclosed verandah, by the flickering light of a hurricane lamp, Ana offered to lend her companions some reading material.

'How long were you expecting to travel, my dear?' asked Madeleine, watching the younger woman extract volume after volume from her satchel.

'I don't like to be without a book,' Ana said. She smiled sheepishly. 'There wasn't much time to pack—I just grabbed whatever was to hand.'

'You must have quite a collection. Rather diverse, too,' added Madeleine, with careful tact. 'It's not often one finds Algernon

Blackwood among poetry primers.' She passed a few items of interest over to the friar.

'My mother doesn't discriminate,' said Ana. 'Anything legible goes on the shelves—there's little else at Halfwell to keep one occupied of an evening.'

'A perfectly laudable pastime,' the friar opined. He reached for a much-handled volume, which turned out to be a language textbook. The words *Primeras Historias* were stamped into the spine. 'Is this how you learned Spanish?'

'Partly,' said Ana. 'I have a couple of books, but there's also a man in Mullewa called Don Armando. He's an old stonemason— from Valladolid, originally. My parents have him out to the station once a month or so, to help me with pronunciation and such.'

'I don't suppose you've ever read any Cervantes?'

Ana shook her head. 'I haven't been able to find any in translation, but Don Armando has promised to lend me a copy of *Don Quixote* when I'm ready.'

'Hullo,' said Madeleine, suddenly. She held an Ann Radcliffe novel open at arm's length, squinting in the lamplight. 'This is missing a page,' she said. 'Just the inside cover, I think, but— here! So is this!' She reached for another. 'If you look closely enough, you can see where the paper has been torn away.'

The others checked the books they were holding.

'You're right,' said Ana, bewilderment rising in her voice as she inspected the binding. 'How odd! I've never noticed it before.'

The friar flicked through the books nearest him.

'It's common enough, really,' he said. 'The first page or two are often removed when a book is retired from library circulation. Or stolen, of course,' he added, drawing a look of mild alarm from Ana.

'If it *was* a thief, he showed some discernment.' Madeleine held a shabby tome open at the first page. '*Rip-Roaring Adventure Tales* seems to have escaped unscathed.'

'Thank God for small mercies,' the friar laughed. 'We must alert the capable young constable at once. Forget the murder—there's a literary critic on the loose!'

Ana frowned. 'You know, I think I *had* managed to forget it,' she said. 'Just for a moment.'

Madeleine climbed to her feet.

'Come on,' she said. 'Let's take a walk. There's nothing like a stroll after dinner to clear the mind. Don't worry,' she added, sensing Ana's obvious reluctance, 'we'll steer clear of the pigsty.'

Her outstretched hand hung in the air for a few moments before Ana took it. Gesturing for the women to go ahead without him, the friar reached for another book and settled back into his hammock. The old, warped wood of the verandah creaked mournfully as they stepped out into the evening.

* * *

Ana breathed deeply.

The still night air was exactly the same temperature as her body, an effect that worked in concert with the darkness to somehow blur the boundaries of the self, so that she could not say with any real certainty where she ended and the world began. Madeleine was close beside her, almost amongst her. For several minutes, the pair walked in silence, sliding through the stubble, letting the boundless whorl of the Milky Way wash over them. When, some murky minutes later, the day's events finally found their way back into Ana's mind, they were softer somehow, diluted by distance.

'Do you think they'll find him?' she asked.

Madeleine considered a moment. 'I don't know much about this black fellow, the tracker —'

'Cooper,' Ana put in.

'But I know Arnold Parkes. I'd say there's a good chance he'll find the murderer. That is,' she went on, her smirk audible through the dark, 'as long as the man is so good as to handcuff himself to the telegraph pole beside the police station with a written admission pinned to his collar and an embroidered shirt bearing the legend "I did it".'

Despite herself, Ana grinned. 'I'm beginning to get the impression,' she said, 'that you don't much care for Detective Sergeant Parkes.'

Madeleine gave a feigned gasp of shock.

'Is there history between you, then?' Ana pursued, a little too eagerly. Her eyes were growing accustomed to the dark, and she searched her companion's face for signs of a story.

'Not in the way you're thinking,' said the older woman. 'You, my dear, read altogether too much fiction. No, no clandestine romance, no revenge plot. No bad blood—nothing like that.'

'What, then?'

'There's really nothing to tell. You've met Arnold. You've met me. He's pompous; I'm stubborn. He thinks a woman's place is in the kitchen. I think an idiot's place is wherever I'm not. There's really not much more to it than that.' She sighed. 'For a long time, though, I tried. I really did try to keep at least a semblance of civility between us, but there are some people you'll never really be able to please. If you keep trying to bend over backwards for them, you'll eventually break.'

She stopped walking. 'I don't think he's a truly bad man,' she clarified. 'He's just one of those people that isn't worth your worrying over. When you get to my age, you'll be able to spot them. The only problem, though, is that you'll be too withered and wrinkled for the knowledge to do you any good—too worn down by love and war and all the other stupid things that humans do to each other.'

Ana took Madeleine's hand in hers.

'I think you're beautiful,' she said. 'I thought that when I first saw you, and I know it now.'

'That's awfully nice of you to say, my dear.' She smiled.

'The best I usually get nowadays is "handsome", and that's a backhanded compliment if ever I heard one. There are far worse things in life, though, than being homely.'

A few minutes passed in companionable silence. The pair walked on through the night, keeping the distant lights of the homestead in sight between the mulga bushes.

'What was the war like?' asked Ana.

'Unspeakable,' said Madeleine. 'Especially on a fine night such as this. With any luck at all, the world has had the sense knocked back into it and you'll never have to worry about such stupid, mindless things.' She stopped to look at her companion. 'What *will* you do, when this is all over?'

Ana was stunned to realise that she'd not given it any thought.

'I don't suppose there'll be much to do,' she said, 'other than to go home.'

'Straight back to the farm?' Madeleine cocked an eyebrow. 'Is there nowhere else you'd rather go?'

'I don't really know. This is the farthest from home I've ever been. I'd love to see the city, though—all those lives.'

Madeleine smiled.

'Were you born at Halfwell?'

'I was born at sea,' said Ana. 'A day's sail west of Geraldton. My father was apparently something of a salesman: he managed to convince my mother to sail from Santiago six months pregnant.'

'What became of them—your birth parents?'

The younger woman's face fell a little as she felt for the familiar weight of her locket beneath her blouse.

'My mother didn't last long. They say she couldn't live in a land with no mountains; she missed home so much that she simply wasted away. My father went mad with grief, threw her body over the back of his horse and rode off into the desert. Neither of them was ever seen again. Not a trace.'

'It must have been horrible.'

'I was too young to remember any of it,' said Ana. 'Too young to even remember their faces—but I do have this.'

Fishing out her locket, she lifted the silver chain over her head, pausing only to detach the few stray curls it had caught before passing it to Madeleine. The older woman accepted the piece with both hands. It was lozenge-shaped, little more than half an inch long, and had clearly never spent much time away from its owner; the filigree fleurs-de-lis in the centre were beginning to wear smooth. Madeleine slipped the catch and the locket sprang open to reveal two small sepia portraits.

On the left, Ana's father stared out from his silver prison with bold, dark eyes, a stiletto-sharp moustache lending strength to what would otherwise have been a rather soft, gentle mouth. The woman opposite him seemed to have been photographed in the act of gazing adoringly at her husband. Her fine chin was tilted at an imploring angle, her full lips parted slightly. Above this, a black cascade of wanton curls framed a face that shone with fierce, desperate beauty.

'They're certainly a fine-looking pair,' said Madeleine, handing the locket back. 'Are these the only pictures you have?'

'That's all they left me. Nothing else: not even a real grave. We built a little cairn at Halfwell, though the ground beneath it is empty, of course. Sometimes, though —' Ana shook her head.

'Go on.'

'You'll only tell me again that I read too many stories,' she said, 'but sometimes I feel that if I were to reach the coast—if I could only smell the sea—perhaps something would come back to me. Some vague memory, no matter how small.'

Madeleine gave her hand a gentle squeeze. 'There, now. That's something to aim for, when you finally manage to wriggle free of dear Arnold's clutches. A nice big target, too; just head west. If nothing else, you'll see a sunset you're not likely to forget.'

Ana laughed. 'I've often heard it said —'

At that moment, though, both women heard something altogether more immediate; the dry, heavy snap of an acacia branch. As one, they whipped round to squint through the scrub. It was difficult to make out anything in the gloom, and neither of them had thought to bring a lantern. On leaving the house, the night had been clear, sunlight still clinging to the corners of the sky; they had wandered for a good while, though, and darkness had long since managed to insinuate itself fully. Shadows hung from the trees, twisting them into strange and unfamiliar shapes. A sudden hush had fallen; so natural to her were the sounds of the bush that Ana could only really identify the low, ambient insect thrum by its abrupt absence. Something had startled even the crickets into silence.

There it was again, softer this time—a careful footstep away in the mulga.

'Who's there?' Madeleine's voice was unexpected, deafening.

No response.

'This'd better not be you playing tricks —' she faltered, forgetting for a moment the friar's anonymity. In the end, she settled on: 'you God-botherer!'

A few seconds of silence followed, during which neither Ana nor Madeleine dared draw breath. Then, finally, a step, then another, and another, retreating swiftly into the night. Ana let go of Madeleine's hand, realising only then that she had been gripping it bloodless, and took off in pursuit. The unknown person was heading east, away from the house, at a rate of knots. The crackling footsteps grew quieter by the second. Breathless, her feet slipping on the uneven dirt, Ana crested a slight rise and pushed through a needling thicket of waist-high wild oats.

The landscape fell away below her, unobstructed, for at least a mile.

There was not a soul in sight.

* * *

The friar was exonerated swiftly enough. His soft shape could be seen on the verandah, silhouetted against the lamplight, from a hundred yards away. He was in his hammock, asleep. As Madeleine and Ana drew closer, they were calmed somewhat by the comforting, quotidian sound of his snoring, the slow rise and fall of the book which still lay open on his chest.

'It was probably just one of the station lads having us on,' opined Madeleine, as she settled her weight onto the creaking sofa. 'Christ only knows how much of that whiskey they've managed to get through by now.'

'All the same,' said Ana, 'I'll be glad to sleep inside tonight.'

Beyond the well of light from the hurricane lamp, the darkness was absolute. Soon enough, Madeleine went inside to prepare their annexed sleeping quarters and check on the party of drinkers. Out on the verandah, Ana picked up the novel nearest her and began again the Sisyphean reading and re-reading of the first sentence to strike her eye. She sat for nearly an hour, trying vainly to rid her mind of the day's creeping horrors, before following her new-found friend inside and crawling into bed at last.

All was still, and the hum of the crickets rose to fill the night once more.

CHAPTER NINE

'It's these blasted motor cars,' said Parkes. 'Fast enough, of course, but without a road—or at least a good, solid path to drive on—they're bloody useless.'

His small audience nodded patiently. It had been almost an hour since the detective sergeant burst through the door, red with sun and fury, to announce that the fugitive had got away.

He was not pleased.

Automobiles were just the latest in his litany of culprits. Parkes had already placed the blame for his quarry's escape squarely at the feet of Cooper ('past his prime'), the weather ('too dry for good footprints') and the God-awful hairstyles embraced by the youth of the day (the connection here was a little unclear, but none of those present had asked him to elaborate, for fear that he might do so). Notably absent was the idea of any relationship between the suspect's escape and the aptitude of the detective sergeant himself, a point which Madeleine Dawson had not missed the opportunity to raise.

By the time Parkes had run through his furious rebuke, the tea had well and truly grown cold.

Spying an opportunity to extricate herself from what had become a thoroughly torturous assembly, Ana rose and reached for the tea tray, offering to brew a fresh pot. The others blinked, as if awakening from a deep sleep. Parkes looked around in surprise.

'No,' he said, slowly. 'No, better not. We'll have to get back on the road if we're to make any headway today.'

One by one, the others stood and stretched.

'Where are we going?' asked Ana.

'You just make sure you have everything packed. We shan't be turning back if you've forgotten anything.' Parkes paused a moment, then smirked. 'That being said, I can think of at least one bag I won't mind leaving behind.'

The object of this parting shot was, of course, Madeleine, who merely observed that if she was to be one of the detective sergeant's cast-offs, she would at least have some decent company in his professional aspirations and sense of dignity, both of which had been abandoned years ago.

Slipping discreetly past the sparring pair, Ana went to gather her books.

* * *

The cabin of the Ford had been cramped enough on the way down from Mullewa, but the addition of Madeleine's sketching-case and Constable Johns's six-foot frame now pushed the prospect of a single trip into the realm of impossibility. After much discussion—veering on more than one occasion into hostile territory—it was decided that Johns and Ms Dawson would take the train back to Geraldton. Having seen the artist safely home, Johns would head to Dongara to rendezvous with the others.

The town of Dongara was an hour or two westwards, boasting a police station sufficiently well equipped for the party to regroup and conduct via telephone and cable such communications as might prove necessary for the next stage of the journey. What, precisely, the next stage of the journey might comprise, none could say—at least, not with any real semblance of accuracy. Ana did know, however, that Dongara lay on the coast, and this quietly thrilling geographic detail was the only thing that went some little way towards ameliorating the sorrow she felt at having to part from Madeleine, so soon after the first flowerings of their friendship.

The friend in question was farewelled in a loose gathering on the back verandah, watched at a wary distance by the landholder and his coterie.

'I don't suppose there's anything else you need from me?' Madeleine asked.

'Your absence will be more than sufficient,' answered Parkes.

Madeleine sighed. 'Very well. I shall have to entrust these to you, Cooper,' she said, passing the tracker her stack of sketches, 'as I'm not sure the detective sergeant is capable of handling them without cutting himself on the edges. I can only assume that's why we've never seen him with a book.'

Ana could almost swear to the fact that she saw the impassive tracker flash a smile, but a fraction of second later, when the detective sergeant spun to glare at him, Cooper's face was stony once more.

'There is, of course, the matter of my fee,' prompted Madeleine. Parkes snorted.

'Take it up with the Assistant Commissioner, if you're so close with him. I'm sure dear "Stevie" won't let you leave empty-handed, though Christ knows you deserve to.'

'I didn't realise that art criticism had been added to your list of talents,' said Madeleine, with feigned surprise. 'Why, that would bring the number of items squarely into the single digits.'

In a superhuman display of self-control, Parkes ignored the gibe.

'Art's got nothing to do with it,' he snapped. 'The fact is, having a picture of the bloke hasn't helped us in the slightest. By the time we've copied it and sent it out for distribution, the murderer could be halfway to Timbuktu. It's not as if someone's going to pop up out of nowhere and say, "Why—that's old so-and-so!"'

'It's Arthur Beynon.'

It took a moment for the rest of the party to register the remark at all—the others had been talking quietly amongst themselves, having long ago lost interest in the interminable Parkes–Dawson feud—and several moments longer to divine its source.

Ana looked at the friar. The friar turned to Madeleine. Madeleine frowned at Parkes. Parkes raised an eyebrow at Constable Johns. Johns simply shrugged.

The only person present who did not appear completely puzzled—and thus, it may be deduced, the person responsible for all the puzzlement in the first place—was Cooper.

'I beg your pardon?' asked Madeleine, looking at the tracker with astonishment.

'That's Arthur Beynon,' he repeated, tapping the topmost sketch.

'What?' Parkes snatched the piece of paper from Cooper's hands and stared at it furiously, as if hoping to find the name hidden amongst the shading in the dead man's hair. 'Damn it, man, why didn't you say anything sooner?'

Cooper shrugged. 'You didn't show 'em to me.'

Parkes roared in anger.

'Who is Arthur Beynon?' asked Madeleine, with slightly more civility.

'He's a salesman,' said Cooper. 'Sells miners lamps and other electric stuff, all up the coast and through the goldfields.'

'Never heard of him,' said Constable Johns.

As it turned out, this was neither an indictment on the young policeman's powers of observation nor the narrowness of his social circle. Indeed, Parkes himself had only ever heard of Beynon in passing, and if it hadn't been for the garrulous Mullewa postmistress, the name would have been completely foreign to Ana and the friar, too.

'But that's awfully odd, isn't it?' said Madeleine. 'I was born in Geraldton, and I've lived in the region more or less my whole life. That's —' she pulled herself up short, modesty preventing her from divulging the exact figure. 'Well, that's a good few years. I know just about everyone from here to Broome. I can even remember the day this sorry creature was born,' she added, with a good-natured wink at Constable Johns. 'Doesn't it seem a little strange that neither Arnold nor I should have managed to make his acquaintance?'

Cooper lifted both palms in total abdication of responsibility.

'I'm not his lawyer,' he said. 'I've only met the bloke once.'

'Where was that?'

'Out past Mount Magnet, early this year. The picture show was in town, and he was trying to flog them some new sort of bulb for their projector.' He thought for a moment. 'Would've been a day or two before Good Friday, I suppose.'

'Was it definitely him, though?' Madeleine pressed. 'Is there a chance you're mistaking him for someone else?'

The tracker's immediate reply was a look of injured dignity. When this didn't work, he resorted to evidence.

'He told me his name,' said Cooper. 'Told *everyone*. Had a little singsong spiel: *Call J. H. Sweetingham and Company—your experts in electricity. Ask for Arthur Beynon, mind—he'll see that you aren't left behind!*'

This performance left its little audience stunned. Cringe-provoking lyrical content aside, it was thoroughly unsettling to see the skill with which Cooper, po-faced as ever, had assumed another man's voice. Everything had been altered: the timbre, the tone, the rhythm of his syllables. Cooper appeared to be a human phonograph.

'Well,' said Madeleine, the first to recover, 'if you ever tire of being bossed around by this boor, a vaudeville career surely beckons.'

The boor tugged at his moustache. 'The question is,' he said, too caught up in the mystery to counterattack, 'who would want to murder an electric lamp salesman?'

There was a long pause.

'Luddites?' suggested the friar, at last. It was an unhelpful offering, but after a few minutes of vague speculation, no-one else had managed to come up with anything much better.

'I suppose we'd better get to Dongara and send the word round,' said Parkes, at last. 'At the very least, we can track down his offices and let 'em know—they can notify the poor blighter's next of kin.'

* * *

The sand was everywhere.

It crept in under the edges of the windowpanes, rattling in their casements. It blew in at the corners of the wind-whipped canopy. It was in Ana's eyes, in her nostrils, under the loose collar of her dress. She coughed, wiping at her face with a sleeve—it came away rust-red and stained with sweat.

They had been driving for three quarters of an hour, but it felt like an eternity. The unsealed road was prone to craters and corrugations, and the vehicle's occupants had long since been jostled numb. Ana toyed for a while with the idea of asking Cooper to slow down, if only to spare them the bruises, but knew that this would mean prolonging the already interminable journey. Passing the time in conversation was impossible; engine noise aside, the swirling sand seemed to seek out open mouths with unerring accuracy. The landscape—what little of it could be caught through dust-caked windows—was unchanging.

Ana clutched at her locket, occupied almost exclusively in trying to prevent her teeth from clashing together. From time to time, convinced that the coast must almost be upon them, she risked pressing her face to the top of the window, hoping to catch the distant glimmer of the ocean. Each time, though, the vehicle's rocking chassis saw her swiftly rebuffed, with nothing but an aching forehead to show for her troubles. Her attempts to catch the soft scent of salt on the air were similarly frustrated by the westerly wind, which offered only sand in its stinging rebuke. At last, she sank down in her seat, exhausted.

It was then, at precisely the moment when she was consoling herself with the thought that things couldn't, in all probability, get much worse, that things got worse.

Suddenly, she was airborne. The whole car was airborne, or at least tilting at an angle thoroughly non-conducive to effective road travel. For a moment, instead of moving through the world, Ana felt as though the world were moving through her. Then the ground hit and shock rendered everything silent. She caught a frozen image, like a poorly posed photograph, of the friar colliding with the ceiling, his face contorted in pain and shock. Slowly, sound returned, the screeching mechanical protest of brakes co-mingling with the wordless cries of the human element in one cacophonous wail. They slid to a halt, the world returning with a thud to its customary place beneath them. The cloud of dirt and detritus kicked up by their tyres hung over the vehicle for a long minute, blood-coloured particles dancing in the feeble breeze before settling gently over the windscreen.

'What in the bloody buggering hell was that?' demanded the detective sergeant.

With a groan of effort, Cooper hauled his body around to check on the passengers in the back. His eyes, wide and white, fixed Ana with a curious look of desperation. Just as suddenly, he snapped out of it; satisfied that neither passenger was in immediate danger of expiring, he cracked the door open and staggered out to assess the damage. Parkes took a moment to stretch his shoulders out, wringing from them an alarming series of percussive cracks before following the tracker outside.

'Still in one piece?' the friar asked Ana.

She nodded, wincing through a little tremor of resultant pain. 'What happened?'

The friar shrugged. 'We must've hit something,' he said. 'Shall we go and take a look?'

Gingerly, they extracted themselves from the murky darkness of the vehicle and stood in the sudden sunlight, blinking. The road stretched from horizon to horizon, a dark, sparse ribbon of dirt splitting the scrub. Clusters of eucalypts punctuated the otherwise empty vista, their olive-green leaves vivid against the red earth. Directly ahead, two parallel lines scored the dirt, reaching out to disappear into the distance: it appeared that the vehicle had spun on impact, such that the travellers were now staring back at their own tracks.

Parkes and Cooper were crouched in front of the car, muttering in low tones as they examined the damage. As Ana drew closer, she saw that Cooper was holding a severed headlamp in one hand, while the detective sergeant struggled with a bent wheel-guard. The issues appeared largely cosmetic, though a dented grille seemed to be causing the tracker some consternation, as it presented a very real possibility of interfering with the crank starter. The little interest that these matters held for Ana was immediately eclipsed when, glancing over the policeman's shoulder, she finally perceived the cause of their crash. Some twenty feet away from the front of the vehicle, at the point where the formerly sure tracks suddenly deviated from their previous bearing, lay the body of a kangaroo.

'Big bastard, isn't he?' grunted Parkes, looking up from the wheel-guard. 'Don't usually get the reds this far south. If you find yourself inclined in any way towards usefulness, padre, perhaps you could drag it off the road. Don't want anyone else taking flight.'

On the other side of the vehicle, the friar was still. For a moment, he seemed about to baulk, but quickly steeled himself to set out through the settling dust. Parkes gave a quietly derisive laugh as he passed, then returned to the mechanical matters at hand.

Ana moved to follow the friar, but a firm hand took hold of her wrist. She turned, bracing herself to receive some arbitrary remnant of the detective sergeant's scorn, but found herself looking instead into the shadowed, solemn eyes of Cooper.

'Tell 'im to do it quick,' he said, softly enough to escape the attention of his commanding officer. Then he was back at the exposed engine, and Ana was left staring at the object he had slipped into her grip—a foot-long spanner, running slightly to rust at the extremities. Pondering the tool's possible uses, she hurried after the friar.

Just as Parkes had said, the kangaroo was a particularly impressive specimen—close to seven feet from tail to tip—if presently in rather a poor state of repair. Several ribs, startling in their whiteness, had been pushed through a ragged hole in the animal's flank by the impact, and one of the great legs had been shattered. Glassy-eyed, it lay silent and completely still.

The friar hummed absent-mindedly, wiping unsteady hands on the homespun of his cassock. Never having been this close to a kangaroo before, he was not at all sure of the best way to proceed. At length, deciding that the thick, rope-like tail presented the most immediate opportunity for a sure grip, he squatted down to take hold of it.

Suddenly, the thing was alive.

The kangaroo kicked out, rolling its broken bulk away from this new menace. There was an awful whistle in every wrecked breath as the wretched thing scrabbled in the dirt, struggling to stand on its sole remaining leg. Ana and the friar staggered back, catching at each other for support as they sought to evade the wildly swinging claws. Somehow, the kangaroo managed to right itself, and careened off at an unstable angle, falling to the roadside once more. It lay there, wheezing horribly, for only half a second before scrabbling up anew and vaulting into the bush. A sea of wanderrie grass swallowed the beast, tangling broken limbs and bringing it to ground for the final time. Mercifully hidden from view, the kangaroo's anguished thrashing carried in the noisome crackle of dry scrub.

Mercy moved the friar to pursuit, but Ana grabbed at his arm. She had seen firsthand the torn bodies of dingoes reckless enough to hunt outside the safety of the pack; she knew the damage that even a single black-nailed kick could deliver.

'You'll share his suffering, if you're not careful.' She held out the spanner. 'Watch out for the feet.'

The friar stood for a moment, feeling the weight of the steel in his hand. The scrub refused to be silent, shaking with the panic of the animal's slow ebb. When the friar finally moved, it was sudden and startling; he fell into the bush as if from a cliff, as though hoping that momentum would carry him where courage would not. As the little figure disappeared from view, Ana could hear him close on the kangaroo, footsteps relayed in the crack and snap of parched wanderrie and wattle.

'Made a break for it, did he?'

The detective sergeant appeared at Ana's shoulder, rubbing engine grease from his hands with an old rag. It was not at all clear whether the subject of his question was mendicant or marsupial. He showed no inclination towards elaborating, and any further discussion was curtailed by the dull, inevitable sound of the friar's mission reaching its end. The silence that followed was something awful—even the raucous cockatoos seemed to have ceased their communion, and the still-fresh horrors of Wongoondy loomed in the minds of everyone present. It was fully two minutes before the friar began to make his way back to the road, and so weary did the little man look upon emerging that Ana immediately ran to embrace him. Parkes hung back, half-formed drolleries stuck in his throat. Words of comfort, though, were harder still to extract, so in the end, his lone offering was the oil rag. It was stiff and mottled, the once-cheery daffodil motif almost obscured by grease.

Taking it, the friar wiped his hands. He trudged towards the car, never lifting his eyes from the red, merciless earth.

CHAPTER TEN

Progress was slow.

Ana kicked at the ground in frustration, knocking loose a large, flat pebble. It tumbled down the broad bank of the Irwin River and into the water, the lazy current carrying it a few feet seawards before finally allowing the poor, displaced thing to settle on its sandy bed.

The friar paused to regard the scene in quiet, blissful contemplation, just as he had stopped a minute prior to watch a wattlebird building its nest, and several moments before that in order to watch a trail of ants struggling with a leaf.

'Oh, do come along!' cried Ana, quite unable to contain her impatience any longer.

The collision with the kangaroo had added more than an hour to their journey, and they had not managed to reach Dongara until nearly five o'clock. The town's high street was a marvel, a cool avenue lined with Moreton Bay fig trees. Their huge, spreading branches plunged tin rooftops into improbable shade, while the clifflike buttress roots made an obstacle course of the roadside. Sheltered at last from the summer sun, the occupants of the battered vehicle felt the collision's queer tension begin to fade.

Ana had been utterly over the moon when Detective Sergeant Parkes had given permission for his wards to take a walk down to the sea, the better to let him focus on the investigation at hand. There was, of course, the caveat that Constable Johns remain with them every moment of the way—the time lost in the crash meant that he had comfortably beaten his superior back to the police station—but it would take a far greater imposition than that to dampen Ana's enthusiasm at the prospect of finally coming face to face with the Indian Ocean. The sea breeze had arisen early in the afternoon, bringing with it the telltale scent of salt, and from the moment the young woman's nostrils had caught it, she had been in a state of near mania.

Ana had set out, then, at speed, fairly skipping down the path behind the police station to the little track that wound its way along the northern length of the river. She would happily have run the whole way to the river mouth and the ocean beyond—a distance of only a mile or so—but it soon became all too apparent that her enthusiasm greatly exceeded that of her companions. The mendicant, it seemed, was glad enough of the freedom, but he appeared to derive his pleasure from the journey, rather than from any prospect of a destination. The bulk of his peregrinations across the continent thus far had been confined to the north-western plains, which offered a wealth of spectacular landscapes, but little in the way of greenery. Hemmed in between the river and the sea, Dongara was striking in its contrast. The friar almost crawled along, glutted with the green glory of creation, letting beauty dampen and dispel the slow horror of the kangaroo's death. For several minutes, he stood transfixed by the glistening gossamer of a spider's web, caught more surely than any scuttling prey; it was only by transferring his attention to the frogs, with their doleful courting chorus, that Ana was finally able to coax him onwards.

If the friar's pace was frugal, though, the constable's was positively glacial.

Out at Wongoondy, he'd had no problem taking on custodial duties—there had been little else to engage his attention, after all—but having now returned to his customary stomping grounds, Johns was constantly being reminded of the hundred-odd happenings which he felt to be far more fruitful uses of his time. He knew, for instance, that several of his old schoolmates would be diving for crayfish that very afternoon while another group were gearing up for a boxing match in the centre of town. Even taking desk duty down at the station would be preferable, as the time spent away from town had enabled him to think of no less than three thoroughly serviceable new excuses for striking up conversations with the report typist. The young lady hadn't shown any interest in his romantic overtures thus far, but Constable Johns was of the firm belief that persistence was the sole precursor to love. His own father had pursued his mother for seven years before she had finally consented to marry him, and theirs was a practically perfect union—they only ever argued on the rare occasions when they happened to find themselves in the same room.

With his train of thought shunted off on such fruitless tangents, Johns mooched along the riverbank, trailing a good twenty yards behind the friar. Ana had, by now, managed to more than double that distance, dashing ahead like a madwoman before turning to wait for the stragglers, her body so visibly racked with pained impatience that a fisherman on the opposite bank was obliged to call over to ask whether he should run for the doctor.

If the concerned angler had still been watching when Ana finally crested the low line of dunes separating her from the sea, he may well have gone running for Doctor Andersen after all.

At the very first sight of her longed-for ocean, Ana broke into a run. Tripping on the scrubby vegetation at the top of the dunes, she toppled down the shoreward slope and fell to the sand, shaking with silent, breathless laughter. By the time the others finally idled their way over to her, she had regained the bulk of her composure, but telltale grains of sand still clung to her cheeks, picking out the moist outlines of tear tracks.

Discomfited by such a blatant display of emotion, Constable Johns took himself off along the beach, feigning a sudden interest in the seaworthiness of a small dinghy some hundred yards away. As long as he was still able to cast an eye over his charges every few minutes, no harm could come of a little distance.

The friar, for his part, was unruffled. With slow, careful movements, he lowered himself to the ground beside Ana, shaking the skirts of his cassock clean of sand. A simple glance left him satisfied that the young woman had sustained nothing in the way of lasting physical injury.

'What do you think?' he asked, gazing out to sea.

Ana sniffed, dabbing at her eyes with an outsized sleeve.

'It's beautiful,' she said. She was telling the truth. The boundless waves exceeded every expectation, the sheer scale of the ocean eclipsing every image conjured by polished shells and fireside stories. Tide-tossed vessels pitched amongst distant whitecaps, propelled by the same raw power which had hewn this wide bay from the coast, slow and inexorable. While the water lapping at her toes was gentle, every little wavelet held a wild promise of distance, of depth, of something incomprehensible and immense.

'And yet?' the friar prodded. He had caught the near-imperceptible shade of discontent in Ana's answer. 'You were expecting something more, perhaps?'

'Why must you always ask questions?' she snapped. The friar had hit a nerve.

It was, of course, quite inevitable that Ana should be disheartened by her first encounter with the coast. What she had been hoping for was nothing less than a miracle. The mute vastness of the water, impressive though it undeniably was, brought her not one step closer to her parents. The fine spray kicked up by the sea breeze smelt of salt and seaweed and little else. Suddenly, Ana found herself furious—furious at her parents for having disappeared, furious at the ocean for keeping their secrets and, perhaps most of all, furious at herself. How could she have been so foolish? How could she have been so naïve as to think that a body of water, no matter how big, could give her the answers she so desperately needed? She was a child—a shamefaced, story-spoilt child—and the mendicant had seen straight through her. Suddenly, her frustration had a target, a target infinitely more assailable than the Indian Ocean.

'Why don't you leave well enough alone?' Ana's voice rose as she warmed to her indignation. 'You're always pushing and prodding, sticking your nose into things that don't concern you in the slightest. Why, if you hadn't gone and wired for the police, I wouldn't have been dragged all the way out here in the first place!'

'And you wouldn't have been disappointed?' suggested the friar, softly.

Ana brought both fists down on the wet sand with a soggy, rather impotent thud.

'¡Ya basta!' she shouted. 'Stop doing that! I'm tired of you pretending that you know me—acting as if you can see straight through me. You can't! You don't know the first thing about me, so take that perverse smile off your lips.'

She lapsed into a brief and furious silence, breathing hotly, hands straying to her locket.

'As a matter of fact,' she realised, giving a sudden start, 'I don't know a thing about you, either! You just popped up out of nowhere, like a thief in the night. Nothing to show for yourself— not even a name. Why should I believe a word you say? You might not be a friar at all. Why, you could've killed that poor man yourself!'

For a minute or two, neither spoke. At the first sound of raised voices, the constable had craned his neck to glance down the beach at them, but as soon as it was evident that no blood would be spilled, he lost interest. There was nothing to hear now but the slow, hissing collapse of the waves and the distant disagreements of a group of gulls. The friar seemed to be lost in thought. He had not managed to rid himself of the perverse smile, but Ana's other concerns must have been taken under consideration, for when next he spoke, his tone was conciliatory.

'You're right,' he said. 'You're absolutely right. Not about me killing anyone, of course—I think you can sense that—but it is true that I've asked for your trust without giving you my own.'

He looked up at the sun, which had begun to sink towards the waves, reddening the western sky. He held up a hand, hesitated as if calculating, then pointed out into the ocean.

'There,' he said.

Ana followed the line of his outstretched finger to the north-west. The sea was vast and empty.

'What's there?' she asked, curiosity and the remnants of anger fighting for control of her voice.

'The first thing about me,' said the friar, grinning. 'The place where I was born—about four thousand miles in that direction, more or less.'

Despite herself, Ana found her curiosity piqued. 'You're not from England, then?'

'My father was English,' said the friar. 'Something of a big name in the admiralty. My mother, though, was from Calcutta, and that's where I was born. She was the daughter of a Bengali merchant—beautiful and rather well-to-do, but that didn't stop eyebrows from going up when it became clear that a child was on the way.'

The friar gave a somewhat bitter little laugh. 'He couldn't marry her, of course. The mixing of races may have been commonplace in the days of company rule, but in Victoria's enlightened times, it was nearly unheard of. Still, he was good to us, in his own way—found a place for my mother among the embassy staff, and as soon as I was old enough, he paid for me

100

to begin schooling with the Jesuits. When he was reassigned to Singapore, several years later, he took us along. In the noise and the crush of the Straits Settlements, no-one seemed to notice us much.'

Ana nodded quietly, wrapped up in the narrative. She gazed out to sea and tried to picture these lands, far beyond the horizon.

'Every few years,' the friar went on, 'my father would receive a new commission and the process would repeat itself. Hong Kong, Burma, Ceylon—new languages, new rules, new ideas. There was really only one constant—the church, stolid and unchanging.' He laughed again. 'You can go into any Catholic church in the world, from Macao to Mozambique, and you'll find the same centuries-old rites, the same dead language. For whatever reason, I loved it. It felt like home to me, more so than the crowded streets of Calcutta, and more so than my father's native land, where we finally ended up. He wanted to retire in Devonshire, you see, on the family estate. While his career was ending, mine was just beginning. I was about the age you are now, and ready to strike out on my own. Trouble was, though, I had nothing.' He held out his empty hands as evidence. 'No money, no skills to speak of, not even my father's name—after all, it's one thing to play at families with a little foreign boy in the tropics, but quite another to give them a seat at the table in Stenholm Hall, with all those ancestors in oils staring down from the walls. One thing I *did* have, though, was an education, so I applied to the seminary.' He smiled. 'It was so peaceful. Nothing but dust and books and contemplation. I worked, I studied, I grew; I was home.'

'What went wrong?' asked Ana.

The friar looked up in a dreamy sort of surprise, having half-forgotten his audience.

'I assume,' the young woman pressed, 'that travelling halfway round the world and living as a nameless vagabond is not in the normal course of priestly progression. There must have been a problem.'

'A problem,' said the friar. 'Yes, of course. The problem, unfortunately, was a very simple one: I didn't believe a word of it.'

It was Ana's turn to look surprised. 'You didn't believe a word of what?'

'Any of it,' the friar shrugged. 'The saints, the scriptures, the catechism. None of it seemed remotely plausible to me.' He laughed. 'I can see I've shocked you with my heresy, but hear me out. My mother was a Hindu. I grew up amongst Muslims, Buddhists, Jains—not to mention the dread disciples of the Church of England! My formative years were scattered across the globe, exposed to a multitude of different beliefs, each one held up as the sole, solemn answer to the questions that plague us all. The natural assumption, of course, is that one's own faith is right and the others are wrong, but I felt—and, in a way, I suppose I still feel—that all of these people must be right, at least in essence. Psalms, hadiths, koans: can they be anything other than different facets, different ways of dissecting the same essential mystery?'

'And what did your teachers think of this theorem?' asked Ana, drily.

'I never breathed a word of it,' said the friar. 'The teachers of the church are fond of study, but less so of learning. True learning requires questions to be asked, and ceremonies do not survive the centuries untouched if questions are permitted. Even so,' he sighed, 'I believe I could've stayed on as a priest quite happily for the rest of my life. I was ordained and given a cosy parish in the countryside. I went through the motions and I brought people comfort. They didn't see me as I was—a conflicted man—but more as a sort of frame upon which to hang the familiar robes of faith.'

He paused, fingering the rough edges of his cassock. Ana ached to take advantage of his sudden garrulousness, to interrupt with one of the thousand questions burning within her breast, but something stopped her. She sensed that he was preparing to go on, almost as if he needed a moment to gather his thoughts, or to gather courage.

'I stayed,' he said at last, 'I stayed in my little village for a good many years, and would have stayed happily for a good many more, but something happened—something utterly devastating.'

'The war?'

'Worse,' said the friar. 'I fell in love.'

Ana gave an involuntary gasp. 'With whom?' she asked, failing utterly to disguise the thrill in her voice.

'The teacher at the village school. We shared an interest, you see, in the world beyond the parish borders—rather a rare thing in that cosy little corner of the county. We'd find excuses to meet: just once a week, at first, after Sunday school, but before long, we were in the vicarage library nearly every evening.'

Here, his voice fell almost to a whisper, and Ana was forced to lean forward in a most undignified way to avoid being left out of the story altogether.

'We had a few shelves of books, a subscription to the *Times* and a faded old globe—hopelessly outdated, especially after the war. We'd sit and compare destinations late into the night, imagining ourselves pushing through a crowded market in Morocco, or watching the fishermen mend their nets somewhere in the Aegean. From the glorious, threadbare comfort of that little room, we read about the revolution in Russia. The very wastes of Siberia seemed romantic, somehow, when lived through candlelight at a lover's side.'

'Did you ever imagine yourself here?' asked Ana.

The friar laughed.

'Not for a moment. It *is* beautiful, though,' he sighed. 'Marion would've loved it.'

'What happened?'

The answer was not immediately forthcoming. For several

minutes, the friar seemed to stare out at the whitecaps.

'We were discovered,' he said, at last. An unfamiliar edge had found its way into his voice. 'We were careless. For years, we'd been safe in the library. Years! Then, one night, we became foolish—a little too much wine, perhaps.' He forced a laugh. 'The fair was in town, you see, and I found myself gripped by a reckless desire to step out in public. There's nothing wrong with a priest taking a stroll around the fairground with one of his parishioners, after all!' Here, he turned a beseeching look upon Ana, as if her support would save him now. 'I don't know what got hold of me. The moonlight, the laughter—where else can I really lay the blame, other than at my own feet?' He sighed. 'It was the mayor's wife that found us. We were under the oak trees, only a hundred yards or so from the lights of the carousel. Just a kiss—just one kiss—but it was enough. Before the sun rose the next morning, they had me on the train, with the understanding that the day I next set foot in the village would be my last.'

Ana's eyes were white and wide.

'But that's awful!' she said. 'Surely the church has some kind of process—a hearing, or trial, or something of the sort?'

'I don't believe the church got the chance to hear of it before I was sent on my way.'

'But —' Ana hesitated, a dozen questions jostling for supremacy. The winner was never really in doubt. 'But what happened to Marion?' she demanded.

The ghastly shadow of a smile settled on the friar's lips. 'Marion,' he said, his voice suddenly small. 'I'm afraid that was the last I ever saw of him.'

The final pronoun fell with considerable force. Ana reeled, reaching for her pendant, the tumult of her thoughts writ large in the flicker of eyelids, the trembling of half-parted lips. Shame, sorrow, sympathy—each of them flashed across her face in split-second succession, as bright and clear as a theatre marquee.

The friar simply sat, subdued, running his fingers through the cooling sand while Ana cast about for something—anything—to say. Nothing in her isolated upbringing had prepared her for a situation remotely akin to this. Words of comfort eluded her, floating just beyond reach in the frenzied silence. The simple task of stringing a sentence together had become something colossal and unassailable.

That moment felt as if it might have gone on forever, but salvation finally came from a most unlikely source. The cry of a klaxon rent the air, and Ana looked up to see Detective Sergeant Parkes waving from the road beyond the dunes, the Ford idling noisily beside him.

'Come on!' he bellowed. 'We need to move!'

Despite the distance, it was clear that the policeman was in a state of great agitation, fairly bouncing from one foot to the other. Cooper sat behind the wheel in calm contrast, as implacable as ever.

Ana leapt to her feet and held out a hand to help the friar up. For a moment, they stood there, unmoving, each holding tight to the other. Ana searched her friend's face, heedless of the impatient horn.

'Thank you,' she said, at last. 'Thank you for trusting me.'

The friar smiled, as if for the very first time. Together, they turned and walked back across the sand.

A hundred yards down the beach, Constable Johns watched the vehicle speed away, shaking his head.

'I suppose I'm bloody walking home, then,' he muttered.

CHAPTER ELEVEN

'He's not dead,' the detective sergeant bellowed as they careened around a corner, his voice elevated by the combined efforts of excitement and engine noise.

'Who isn't?' yelled Ana, clinging to the seat in front of her.

'Beynon! The dead man!'

These seemingly contradictory statements were eventually untangled, but only to the accompaniment of a great deal of interference, interjection and general disagreement. In the interests of clarity and narrative flow, a more succinct precis is provided below.

While his charges were making their way down to the beach, Parkes had returned to the police station. Armed at last with an identity, he had placed a call to J.H. Sweetingham & Company, manufacturers and wholesalers of fine electrical wares, informing them that Arthur Beynon, their sales representative for the northern and coastal regions, had met with an ignominious end. For the sake of both formality and forensics, he had requested that all available information on the man be cabled through to the station at once. Then, pausing only to acquire a pot of fresh tea and a cigar, he had sat down to build a profile of the unfortunate victim.

'Beynon was a total madman,' he summarised, for the benefit of his passengers. 'He was on the road for more than three months at a time, with only a week's break between each trip. On his last jaunt, he went all the way up the coast from Fremantle to Carnarvon—nearly six hundred miles, mind you—and then back down through the goldfields.'

This trip was made all the more astounding by dint of being conducted wholly via horse and cart: despite Arthur Beynon's well-honed sales patter about technology lighting the way to the future, he had evidently been unwilling to embrace the internal combustion engine.

'It looks as if he sold bulbs and filaments to general stores and garages, for the most part, with a sideline in motor components for fishing vessels. That's on the coast, mind you,' clarified Parkes, somewhat unnecessarily. 'On the way back down, he managed to make it through just about every one of the larger stations and mining towns, moving electric lamps by the crateful. Much safer than the old gas lanterns, they say.'

This amount of merchandise, of course, could not be accommodated in a single sulky—the bulk of Beynon's load was demonstration stock. Once a purchase had been arranged, a system of regularly scheduled telegrams enabled the warehouse team in Fremantle to dispatch all stock within two days of the order being placed.

It was at this point in the retelling that the detective sergeant's audience began to protest. They still had not been told where they were going—or, perhaps more pressingly, why—and were unable to see the merit in sitting through a brief but thorough commercial history of north-western electrical hardware distribution.

In response, Parkes handed a single piece of paper into the rear of the vehicle and waited wordlessly for his critics to reach their own conclusions. They peered at it, squinting in the dim, dusty air. It was a typewritten sheet of dates, locations and quantities. The haste with which it had been compiled was clear in the numerous spelling errors, none of which had been struck out or retyped.

It took Ana a few moments to realise what she was reading: the most recent record of Arthur Beynon's sales. The full implication of the evidence did not become clear, however, until she reached the final date, at the bottom of the page.

'November the twenty-seventh!' she exclaimed.

'Today,' said Parkes, for the sake of exposition.

At the same time that Beynon's remains had been hauled out of reach of the hogs, a telegram was dispatched to the Fremantle office in his name. It had been sent from Three Springs, some fifty miles south of his resting place.

Ana stared at the paper in disbelief. 'But how? What on earth could it mean?'

'We're about to find out,' said Parkes. 'Take another look at the records. He sold half a dozen electric lanterns and a crate of batteries to the general store in Port Denison on the morning of the twenty-fifth.'

'Where's Port Denison?' asked the friar.

'Here,' said Cooper.

With an abrupt shudder, the engine fell silent.

* * *

The Port Denison general store was a squat limestone building with iron-barred windows. A wooden sign out the front advertised ice-cream for a penny, and a couple of small boys could be seen working the wooden churn in the shade beside the front door. The overwarm crowd of attendant youngsters parted reluctantly to allow Parkes and his entourage to enter. Displaying the healthy curiosity befitting their age, several of the children hung from the barred windows, peering at the goings-on inside. The detective sergeant sent them packing, and they ran off to play on the closest of the two jetties, taking turns to push each other into the water.

'What can I do for you?' asked the store's proprietress.

She was a stocky woman with a somewhat stern expression, though her voice was shot through with a tone of laconic amusement. She gave the impression, somehow, of being much larger than she was. Overall, a rather formidable woman.

Parkes handed over Madeleine's sketch. Unhurriedly extracting her spectacles from beneath the counter, the shopkeeper gazed at the image for some time.

'That's young Beynon, if I'm not mistaken. Not a brilliant likeness, but it's him.'

The detective sergeant's moustache twitched in undisguised pleasure at this condemnation of his antagonist's work, but he swiftly quelled it and went on with the questioning.

'Would you say you knew him well?'

The shopkeeper tilted her head in a noncommittal gesture. 'Well enough. Comes in every three months, like clockwork. Always the same nonsense.' She slipped into that gruff, rather unflattering tone of voice often used by older women to imitate young men. *'J.H. Sweetingham and Company—your experts in electricity.* As if I've never heard it before, or have any alternative suppliers out here to whom I might give my business.'

Out of the corner of her eye, Ana noticed the friar suddenly stand a little straighter; rather like a dog who has caught a far-off sound, imperceptible to its master.

'When was the last time you encountered him?' Parkes went on.

'The day before yesterday.'

'Did he seem different, in any way?'

The shopkeeper considered this a moment. 'A little rushed, perhaps.' Her voice was measured. 'He was happy, for once, with the order I gave him. Didn't try to sell me an electric pot stirrer, or any other such nonsense.'

'And it was definitely him?' pressed Parkes.

The shopkeeper looked at him for a long moment with a sort of calm concern. 'It certainly wasn't the King of Sweden.'

With some difficulty, Parkes marshalled his patience. 'There was no question of his identity being—obfuscated, somehow?'

'He looked the same as every other time I've seen him,' she said. 'Down to the socks and shirtsleeves, I'm sure. He wore a beard and moustaches, but kept them under control—nothing like whatever it is you have going on there.'

This exhausted the detective sergeant's reserves of tolerance. He rapped out his final few questions, received the terse answers with little grace, and strode out of the shop without waiting for his entourage. Watching him go, the shopkeeper gave the first hint of a smile.

Ana and the friar were now alone on the shop floor, Cooper having elected to wait in the car rather than risk being on the receiving end of the establishment's intolerance. Ana suspected that the detective sergeant would take some time to walk off his anger, giving her a few precious minutes in which to look around the shop. The outlets in Mullewa may have been larger, but she had rarely been inside them: her mother usually elected to have goods delivered directly to the station.

The proximity of Port Denison to the coast gave an intriguing nautical slant to much of the merchandise, and a great many of the items looked as though they must have been imported. Ana ran her fingers over the unfamiliar accents punched into the steel of a French gas lantern, letting her imagination run away with her.

The friar's interests, though, were altogether closer to home.

'Excuse me,' he said to the proprietress. 'Would you mind telling me what this says? I've forgotten my spectacles.'

The stout woman ran her eyes doubtfully over the cassock, shabby sandals and incongruous grin before finally following the little man's line of sight to the side of a wooden packing crate.

'It says "Wyndham",' she said. 'Full of fresh-caught crayfish, that is.'

'Wyndham—that's a town, is it?'

'Of sorts. Just a couple of pubs and a port, really, way up past Broome. Wouldn't exist at all if it weren't for the mines.'

'And how does one spell "Wyndham"?' the friar wanted to know. 'I often find,' he added, by way of explanation, 'that names out here in the colonies are subject to a rather amusing process of transformation.'

The proprietress, for her part, did not appear to be in the least amused. 'We're not a colony anymore,' she said, shortly. 'And we spell it the usual way.'

'Indulge me.'

Seeing no other way of escaping the conversation, she obliged, letter by letter. The friar's response was so enthusiastic that it could only have been feigned—his face fairly lit up, and he shook the shopkeeper's hand with an unaccountable excess of vigour.

'Thank you! You've no idea the help you've given me.'

The stout woman grimaced, sure that she was the subject of some obscure jape. 'Let it not be said that I leave my customers wanting,' she muttered. 'I don't suppose that you will, in fact, turn out to be a customer?'

The friar took the insinuation well. 'Now that you mention it,' he said, withdrawing a tatty purse from his satchel, 'there are some things I've been needing. I'll take a pencil, an envelope and a book of stamps, if you please. My young companion will no doubt be eager to write to her parents and I have some correspondence of my own to attend to. After that, perhaps,' he added, with a wink in Ana's direction, 'some ice-cream?'

* * *

They found Parkes standing at the end of the jetty, kicking listlessly against the weathered wood. Cooper sat on the boards beside him, dangling his legs over the edge and watching the fish in the water below.

'I can't understand it at all,' the detective sergeant confessed. 'First he's dead, then he's alive, then dead again, and now—well, who on earth knows?' He shrugged, defeated. 'We'll all have to take the next train down to Fremantle, I suppose. I can't see any other way to cut through this mess.'

Cooper looked up, something like alarm in the set of his usually stoic features.

'What about me, boss?'

'Naturally, you'll come too,' said Parkes. 'You never know when a tracker'll come in handy. You used to live in Perth, didn't you?'

Several emotions fought for control of Cooper's face, but none retained supremacy long enough for those watching to glean anything.

'Only for a year or two, ages ago. You'd be better with a Noongar bloke, down that way,' said the tracker, cautiously. 'I don't know the place like they do.'

'Nonsense,' Parkes clapped him heartily on the shoulder, nearly knocking the poor man into the sea. 'When it comes to seeking out a trail, there's none better than Cooper—I've always said so. Of course you'll come.'

For a moment, it seemed as if the tracker was about to protest. At any rate, it seemed that way to Ana and the friar; to the detective sergeant, who had already turned back along the jetty, the thought of a command being disobeyed seemed simply inconceivable.

Soon enough, the moment passed. With a sigh, Cooper pulled himself to his feet and joined the others.

CHAPTER TWELVE

Ana lay her head against the heaving frame of the carriage and gazed out of the window.

The world outside, dimming now with the onset of night, rushed past at speeds unable to comfortably comprehend. At this rate, she thought, they might indeed stand a fighting chance of reaching Fremantle before the fugitive lamp salesman, whoever he might turn out to be. A solitary ghost gum approached, looming white in the darkness. In the space of a single moment, it grew from a distant speck to tower over the train before flitting from existence altogether, limbs lifted to the stars in bleached entreaty.

It was Ana's very first time inside a train, and her expectations had been high. She had pictured a sleek, sophisticated thing, the kind that might be seen sweeping out from beneath the marble façade of the Gare du Nord, a miracle of modernity. She had imagined high tea in the dining car, the starched, immaculate collars of conductors and attendants.

This composite mental image, drawn as it was from novels and magazine photographs, was several years and many thousands of miles removed from the great shaking thing now propelling her southwards. Perhaps the biggest discrepancy, though, between expectation and reality was not visual but aural.

In her books, railway carriages were comfortable, leather-scented salons where light conversation might be conducted, something like a drawing room on wheels. Ana had been rather shocked, then, standing at the Dongara railway station, to realise that she could hear the train approaching before she could see it. The whistle split the air, startling into silence the flock of sulphur-crested cockatoos that had been noisily and happily tearing a nearby fig tree to shreds. As the engine grew closer, the ground shook; the steel of the rails began to rattle against the sleepers, a din which built to an almost unbearable level before being eclipsed by the rhythmic roar of the engine itself.

The interior of the carriage was scarcely any quieter, seeming to be composed almost entirely of things that were just mobile enough to be rattled against their neighbours. Windowpanes shook in their steel housings, the bolts fixing the seats to the floor railed against their threads and the dim electric light globes seemed to wish themselves free of their ceiling fixtures. Still, this unsettled symphony was as nothing compared to the human element.

The interior of the train, in stark contrast to the near-desolate emptiness of the surrounding terrain, was seething with activity. A shift on the mines must have ended—in Cue, perhaps, or Mount Magnet, or far out at Paynes Find—for the carriage that Ana and her companions boarded was full of men in various stages of revelry. Some had changed into travelling clothes, but many still wore denim and dungarees. Very few, it seemed, had had the time or the inclination to wash, their faces still grimy with sweat-tracked dirt.

The attitudes of the miners ranged from thorough weariness, several having fallen asleep in their seats, to undiluted jubilation at finally finding themselves above ground and in states of relative solvency. One or two of the revellers exhibited momentary displeasure upon seeing a uniformed officer board the train, but Parkes soon put their fears to rest by making his way to a booth at the far eastern end of the carriage and seating himself with his back to the rest of the occupants. He, too, was work-weary, and had no desire to investigate what would surely prove to be several dozen minor legal infractions. Ana, Cooper and the mendicant quietly joined him and were presently forgotten by the small number of their fellow travellers who had managed to notice them at all. As the train crept once more towards its former velocity, a couple of fiddles were produced and the festivities began slowly to regain their momentum.

Ana soon found that the volume of both engine and occupants made conversation all but impossible. She tried for a time to read but the constant bucking and jarring of the vehicle interfered with her concentration. Much to her shock, she saw that Parkes and Cooper, seasoned rail travellers both, had managed to fall asleep. Impossible though it seemed at first, the young woman followed them into slumber some half an hour later, the cumulative exhaustion of the day's events finally catching up with her. The little friar, tired though he was, found himself unable to do the same. Some of the miners' restless energy had seeped into him and he couldn't help but be caught up in the thrill.

The jubilation was cacophonous. What the fiddlers lacked in finesse, they made up for in vigour and the enthusiastic accompaniment of the audience, who enlisted the aid of any percussive surface they could find, thumping boots and palms against travelling-cases, thighs and the floor of the carriage itself. Meanwhile, those miners not musically inclined sought out other forms of entertainment. Card games were the initial focus, but the friar's attention was soon drawn to a group of a dozen or so of the men forming a loose circle. After a discreet wander down the aisle to ensure that the detective sergeant was truly asleep, one of them—a leanish, foxy-looking fellow distinguished by the fact that he had made the effort to wash and change into a tweed suit before boarding the train—drew from his jacket a slim wooden paddle, worn smooth with use. One of his companions took out first one old penny, then another, polishing the obverse with a corner of his linen shirt until the bare expanse of Edward VII's forehead shone in the dim light.

They were preparing for a game of two-up.

The friar had only seen it played once before, several months earlier. Then, in a sandy, firelit circle on a Kimberley cattle station, the backdrop had been the seemingly endless stretch of the night sky. Here, in the crowded confines of the railway carriage, the game seemed a study in chaos.

'Come in, spinner!' came the call.

The clamour of the crowd, already overwhelming, rose to fever pitch. The friar was at too great a distance to make out the result of the throw, but the raucous cries from the crowd left him in no doubt as to who the winners were.

Again and again the process was repeated. More liquor was added to the mix, and wealth began to be redistributed in greater quantities. The bets had begun with coins and banknotes, but soon the miners were pulling grains of pure gold from their rucksacks. One old fellow produced a nugget larger than his thumb, which he promptly lost, to thunderous applause. He took a drunken swing at the victor, and for a moment, the watching friar was afraid that he might find himself detained as a witness in a second murder case. Violence was swiftly averted, however—the old man being placated with a tin flask of rum— and the game soon resumed.

After some two dozen rounds, the friar began to lose interest. The noise was familiar enough now to fade into the background, and the rhythmic clacking of the train tracks conspired with the heat of the carriage to sink him into a sort of dull drowsiness.

When he was finally jolted back to full consciousness, it was not due to noise but, rather, its sudden absence. He lifted his head to see the twenty-odd men frozen in a bizarre tableau, staring at the floor, shocked into stillness. The spinner stood dumbly, paddle still extended, mouth agape.

'Where the bloody hell's it gone?' yelped one of the punters, at last. 'I've got five pound riding on that!'

Awoken from their stupor, the others began clamouring. It wasn't hard for the friar to piece together what had happened. Some of the miners were on hands and knees, scrabbling under the seats, while others ran up and down the aisle, looking for the runaway coin. One of the pennies, it seemed, had come up 'heads', while the other had somehow managed to disappear completely from the face of the earth.

'It's not up there, Bill,' said one prospector, addressing a companion who had clambered atop his seat and started to examine the overhead luggage racks. 'I saw it fall.'

'Did ya hear it hit the ground?' asked another.

One man swore he had heard exactly that, while two or three more argued with equal vehemence that no such sound had occurred at all. The search continued for a minute or two, the miners exploring increasingly unlikely corners of the carriage, before curiosity gave way to suspicion. Soon enough, one of the more astute members of the assembly recalled the age-old investigative law of *cui bono*—which of them, he asked, would benefit from the sudden disappearance of a coin? On the last two throws, he pointed out, both coins had landed with the late monarch's face on full display. If this were to happen a third time, the spinner would win all the round's wagers in their entirety. If, on the other hand, the result was one 'heads' and one 'tails', play would continue and he would be none the richer. The obvious conclusion was summed up rather succinctly by a man in dusty, oversized overalls:

'Yer a cheatin' bastard, Jack!'

The spinner stared dismissively down the length of his accuser's outstretched finger.

'You dunno what you're on about,' he scoffed.

Immediately, the crowd erupted. Both the spinner and

his accuser had supporters in sizeable numbers, though their individual accusations and counterclaims were lost to the general clamour. As tensions rose, old grievances grew to overtake the matter at hand and a dozen half-remembered quarrels resurfaced.

From his seat, the mendicant watched in some trepidation. He had no wish to see the simmering tensions boil over into physical violence, but his desire to remain at no small distance from said violence was greater than his spiritual compulsion to counsel for peace. In the end, he contented himself with the familiar comforts of a quiet prayer. Despite his professed lack of faith, some distant saint must have been receptive to his supplications, for the situation was resolved before the first punch could be thrown.

The man who had first pointed the finger of blame had by now exhausted his capacity for rhetoric. Being more inclined to action than to words, he realised that his chances of winning his argument with the spinner would be infinitely improved if his opponent were to lose consciousness. In view of expediting this outcome, he readied himself to unleash the same powerful right hook that had served him so well in previous disputes. Those encounters, though, had been in rather less confined quarters. As he drew back, preparing to strike, the train lurched slightly, sending several of the other men staggering into him. They collided and fell to the floor in a tangle of dusty limbs, the would-be pugilist splayed comically on top. Stunned and winded, the man struggled to right himself, legs flailing in the manner of a toppled cockroach; the laughter of his comrades was less than encouraging. A second or two later, though, all those present were shocked into silence, and even the mendicant found himself leaning forwards in his seat. The downed man's boots protruded ludicrously from the rolls of gathered fabric at the end of his enormous trousers, swinging upended in the air. The boots, however, were not the most notable thing to emerge from his cuffs. At an almost leisurely pace, a polished penny rolled from its denim hideaway down the man's upstretched leg and clattered to the floor, where it spun several times before coming to rest with the regal visage obscured.

The roar of the crowd was all the more overwhelming for the silence that had preceded it. The friar, however, paid it no heed. He had turned back to the occupants of his own seat, still improbably asleep.

'Of course,' he breathed, the light of revelation in his eyes.

Outside, in the dark, another anonymous town rushed past.

* * *

Ana woke in the early hours of the morning. Her sleep had been shallow and fitful, scored with the ominous sound of unseen swine, and she woke less than refreshed. Slowly returning to reality, she took in her surroundings.

The train had stopped at Midland Junction, mere miles from the outskirts of Perth, and now sat seething in its own vapours as passengers jostled to switch lines. The bare electric lights on the station platform illuminated a tangle of lines stretching off into the darkness. Nearly every railway route in the state of Western Australia passed through Midland Junction. Travellers shook themselves from sleep and sought their next trains, some heading for the city centre, others up to the heights of the Darling Range or out to Kalgoorlie, deep in the interior, where the world's longest stretch of dead-straight railway waited to whisk them across the treeless expanse of the Nullarbor to the cities of the east.

Ana shuffled off the carriage, her drowsy eyes roaming over the cluster of tracks, struggling with the somnolent realisation that an unbroken line of steel now connected her to Adelaide, thousands of miles away, and beyond that to Melbourne and the almost mythical metropolis of Sydney, impossibly distant. There she stood, overwhelmed by light and sound and distance, till the detective sergeant returned from the station office and thrust a ticket into her hand.

'Come on,' he grunted, striking out for the other side of the platform.

Shouldering what little luggage they had, the others followed, negotiating the sparse sea of groggy fellow travellers. Even in this pre-dawn darkness, the station hummed—with human activity, of course, but also with engines and electricity, with the aimless thronging of midges among lights that shone the whole night through.

Only one train showed any inclination towards imminent movement, its hydraulics hissing and crackling with impatience; it was towards this that they headed. Obeying some ineffable discretion, Parkes bypassed the first two carriages, hauling himself through the waiting doorway of the third and disappearing into the darkness within. Ana was just behind him, but the moment she grasped the handrail, a shout rang out.

'Oi! Hold it!'

She froze, instantly assuming culpability—she had been raised Catholic, after all—and turned to see a uniformed guard hurrying across the platform. The guard's objective, though, was not Ana, but one of her companions. He made straight for Cooper, grabbing the tracker roughly by the arm.

'Let's see your pass,' he said.

Nothing about Cooper's mien or manner indicated that he was in any way surprised by this treatment. His expression was one of frustrated resignation, his mouth shut firm against the escape of protesting words. In his lieu, it was the friar who spoke.

'We all have tickets,' the quondam holy man said.

The guard gave the rough-robed little figure a dismissive glance before returning to his quarry. He plucked the ticket from Cooper's fist and stared at it like a banker seeking to thwart a forgery.

'No pass, eh?' he said. 'How did you get hold of this? It's well after curfew.'

The indigenous man kept his silence.

'We're all travelling together,' said Ana, finding her voice at last. 'Please, this is the first we've heard about a curfew.'

The guard turned to her and his face underwent a remarkable transformation. Taking in her lace-collared dress, silver locket and charmingly arranged curls, he became, in an instant, a human being. He relinquished his hold on Cooper's arm and smiled. His voice changed, too, softening a little.

'I'm sorry, miss. Of course, you've just come in from up Geraldton way, so it's quite understandable that you might not be aware of the latest legislative developments, so to speak. The changes only went through in March, after all.'

'And what changes might those be?' asked Ana, with arch sweetness.

'The city centre's a prohibited area for Aborigines,' said the guard. 'And there's a curfew all across town. They've gotta have a native pass to be out after six.'

Ana's hand rose to her mouth. 'But that's not fair!' she gasped. 'That's awful!'

The friar was inclined to agree; being rather more experienced in the realm of man's inhumanity to man, however, he eschewed moral objections in favour of the technical.

'We're not going to the city centre.' He held aloft his ticket. 'We're going to Fremantle.'

The guard's face became granite once more. 'The train still passes through Perth station,' he said.

'If we don't leave the train until Fremantle, do we need a native pass?'

'*You* don't need a native pass at all.' The guard jerked a thumb in Cooper's direction. 'He does. And until he has one, he will not be boarding this train. First daylight service is at five thirty— that'll have a carriage for blacks.'

Before the exchange could progress any further, an enormous moustache emerged from the dim interior of the carriage, trembling in irritation. Behind it was the detective sergeant.

'Loath though I am to intrude upon this knitting circle, this train departs in two minutes, and —'

Catching sight of the guard, Parkes brought himself up short. 'What's all this?'

Ana, the mendicant and the guard began to speak all at once. Cooper was silent, looking as though he wanted to slip between the train and the edge of the platform and disappear. After a few seconds, Parkes had heard enough. Removing his credentials from his shirt pocket, he stomped down on to the platform and thrust them in the other man's face.

'I am investigating a fantastically brutal murder,' he said, his voice low and deliberate. 'If this train leaves without me—or any one of my companions—there may well be another. Do I make myself clear?'

The guard hesitated a moment, glancing from the proffered papers to the quivering moustache above them. Despite the statement's technical ambiguity, there was no doubt in his mind that he was being threatened. It was four in the morning and he'd been on duty for nearly twelve hours. There was no functional incentive for him to press the issue. He sighed.

'I'm sorry for the trouble, sir.'

The apology was addressed solely to Parkes. Unwilling or unable to meet Cooper's eyes, the guard simply held out the confiscated ticket. Cooper took it and vanished into the carriage. The others followed, making their way along the cramped aisle to the seats the detective sergeant had saved for them. The mendicant heaved his satchel into the overhead rack and lowered himself into his seat. Ana was just about to do the same when she realised that Cooper had not stopped with them—he was striding on towards the door at the end of the carriage. She moved to follow him, but Parkes laid a hand on her forearm.

'Give him some time.'

With a heavy sigh, Ana acquiesced.

'That was horrible,' she said. The others nodded.

'Some human tendencies are universal,' said the mendicant. 'Love, hate—the best and the worst of them, really.'

'That sort of thing wouldn't happen up north,' opined Parkes. The mendicant cocked his head. 'What makes you say that?'

'Well, everyone knows me up there, for a start,' the detective sergeant said.

His audience shared several seconds of blank confusion before the truth dawned.

'That's what you found unacceptable?' Anger edged Ana's voice. 'Your authority being questioned?'

'Well, if I'd known they were going to be so precious about it, we could've telegraphed ahead—they would've had one of those native passes waiting for us when we got here.'

'He shouldn't need a pass!' the young woman snapped. 'Surely that's the point.'

Parkes gave an indulgent smile. 'Ah, don't let old Cooper sway your judgement. He's one of the good ones—few and far between, they are.'

'He must have known,' murmured the mendicant. 'That's why he was so reluctant to travel south.'

The detective sergeant nodded. 'I reckon you're right. Still, he did the right thing in the end. No complaints. I told you—one of the good ones.'

With nothing left to say, Ana turned her face to the window.

Outside, the guard had managed to corner another unfortunate soul, a tall, well-dressed man with skin no darker than Ana's own; Parkes would've called him a half-caste, perhaps. It was enough to place him in violation of the curfew, at any rate. He had evidently not had the plain good sense to be in the employment of a bellicose officer of the law, an oversight that would now see him miss his train. With a slight jolt, the engine began to move. Ana watched the station grow small and slide away into the night.

CHAPTER THIRTEEN

The sun was rising as they reached the coast.

Perth had passed in near darkness, a vague sense of looming structures and the half-heard sounds of a city beginning to stir. Enclosed within the carriage, Ana had caught only fleeting glimpses but the scale was something shocking. Despite the early hour, there were more cars and carriages on the move than she had seen in the whole of her life. Not for the first time, she wondered how people could live in such number.

She was aware, too, that Perth was on the smaller end of things, as far as cities were concerned. After passing through, she found the idea of London or New York even harder to fathom, let alone the chaos of Bombay or Shanghai. Almost as strange was the lingering stretch of the suburbs, which seemed to creep along the train line like some climbing vine from the tropics. In her experience, towns rose from the scrubland, discrete and self-contained, clustered around a single central street: they were separated from one another by miles of desert or pasture, sometimes a full day away from the nearest settlement.

Perth, though, was different. After the city centre's stone-hewn monuments had been left behind, the train was still pursued by rows of terrace houses, by hotels, churches and stores in sizes and specialties that boggled the mind. Here and there, the sprawl would fade away, replaced by stands of pines or a tangle of untamed bush, but as soon as Ana thought that the city might be behind them, another street of houses would burst forth, another corner shop, another cluster of factories and market gardens.

And then, at last, there was the water.

Less than twenty-four hours after first laying eyes upon it, the Indian Ocean felt like an old friend. The western sky was wide and cloudless, forced to blush by the distant splendour of the sunrise, its glory reflected in the softly shifting mirror of the sea below.

'Marvellous, isn't it?'

The detective sergeant spoke with a sort of proprietary pride, as though he might have had a hand in the arrangement of the continents, or put in a good word with the cosmos as to the best shades for a sunrise. Ana could only muster a wan smile in response. She was still coming to terms with the casual way in which Cooper had been reclassified into something distant, something unacceptable. She stole a glance at the tracker; he was sitting six or seven rows away, staring out of the window, his back straight, his head unbowed. Ana was moved to go and speak to him. She stood, but the resolve left her the moment she stepped out into the aisle. What could she say?

'Have you heard,' said the friar, appearing noiselessly at her shoulder, 'of a man named Joachim Neumann?'

Ana blinked at the unorthodox opening. Forgetting her mission, she allowed herself to be led to a seat on the opposite side of the carriage.

'No,' she said, after a moment's thought. 'It sounds German. Did he have something to do with the war?'

The friar smiled. 'No, I'm afraid he resides rather further in the past. In the seventeenth century, in fact, not far from Düsseldorf. As well as being a musician and a preacher, he was also a rather splendid example of what might be termed, in today's vernacular, a social climber.'

Ana nodded slowly, unsure of how else to respond.

'The fashion of the time, you see, was for people to downplay contemporary culture in favour of the ancients and their lofty ideals—the ideals they saw as acceptable, of course,' he added hastily. 'The thinkers of the renaissance were swift enough to shed those concepts which might be morally troubling—the pederasty, of course, and the promiscuity—along with those that were less politically welcome, such as democracy. Slavery managed to stay the course, somehow.' The friar gave his smile a sardonic twist.

'In an effort to avoid being seen as parochial, Joachim Neumann decided to change his name, swapping it for a Greek equivalent. His son, of course, carried the appellation, too, and by the time his grandson was born—also named Joachim— the family was firmly entrenched in their new identity. This grandson gained some little renown as a hymn-writer, his compositions being so popular that they were translated from German into the other great languages of the continent, and even into our own tongue. Though it is more popular with the Protestants, you may, perhaps, be familiar with "Praise to the Lord, the Almighty"?'

Ana did not appear to be familiar with the song, but this did little to deter the mendicant.

'When writing his hymns, Joachim the younger would often look, like so many of us, to nature for inspiration. One of his favoured retreats was a valley—or *thal*, as it was known in the German of the time—of a rather rugged beauty, through which the river Düssel runs. So great became his association with this valley that it was renamed in his honour, some two centuries after his death. They didn't use the name "Neumann", of course, but the new Greek calque, "Neander", so that the valley is now known as the Neanderthal. I can see that the name is familiar to you,' he said, noting the young woman's involuntary start of recognition. 'You doubtless came to hear of it, though, not through the hymns of the erstwhile Joachim Neumann, but through a scientific curiosity which has found its way into newspaper headlines and adventure stories alike in recent decades.'

'The caveman?' said Ana.

'Indeed—the skeleton of a being, it appears, who walked amongst our earliest ancestors.' The friar smiled. 'The elder Neumann, who hoped to be associated with the great heights of Greek thought and the "new man" of the renaissance, now lives only as a memory tethered to the fossils of the Neanderthal, a man forty thousand years his senior. A man whose very existence threatens the tenets and timelines of Joachim Neumann's faith. A man, in fact, whose entire species faltered and fell into obscurity, eclipsed by those early humans who were able to embrace the working of metal, the building of boats, the exchange of manners and technologies with distant cultures.'

'Why are you telling me this?' Ana said. Then, seeming to realise too late that she had actually voiced the thought aloud, she added: 'It's a fascinating story, of course. I was just wondering what brought it to mind.'

The friar lifted innocent hands. 'You must forgive my ramblings on the vagaries of history. I merely find it somewhat risible that one who sought to become a new man, so caught up in the prejudices of his own time, became instead the name of the oldest savage now known to science.' There was a gentle humour in his eyes. 'I suppose I find it comforting, too, to reflect on the way that ideas change. You were saddened, weren't you, to see the way the world views poor Cooper?' He didn't wait for an answer. 'You're a gentle soul, Ana, and kinder than most. When you look at Cooper, you don't see the differences—only the similarities.'

'Well,' said Ana, 'Cooper and I are certainly much more similar than—oh!'

Through the shuddering window, she saw the ground fall away.

The train swept out above the mouth of the Swan River, supported on a wooden span not much wider that the engine itself. Thirty feet below, sparkling like flung diamonds in the nascent light, the river opened into a narrow harbour, lined on either side with ships of all descriptions. The bridge had been newly rebuilt after collapsing in the floods of the previous year, a fact which the passengers were all the better for not knowing, given how fragile the shaking span felt. As it was, however, they reached the other side with no incident other than the brief and happy commotion caused by the sighting of several dolphins circling below. Moments later, the train was pulling into the terminus at Fremantle.

* * *

Ana stared up at the wide, white ceiling. She couldn't sleep.

All through that long night of travel—the hours spent folded into train seats, the rattling that shook the very thoughts free of her skull—she had ached for a bed. Now that she was finally beneath the blankets, though, sleep refused to come. It wasn't that her tiredness had left her. Fatigue still weighted every muscle, made a foggy mess of her mind, but alongside it was something else. Something buzzing, something urgent, almost like the static of an improperly tuned wireless. It hovered at the edge of her awareness, driving away the sweet solace of sleep, offering in return only the vague and relentless idea that there were things to be addressed.

It certainly didn't help that the sun was now high in the sky, overwhelming the delicate lace curtains and setting the white-walled room aglow. Ana's window faced east. She was on the top floor of the Orient Hotel, three storeys up, in one of the better chambers the establishment had to offer. The bed was as large, clean and comfortable as any to be found in the port city, but its occupant could not bring herself to lie still for long enough to appreciate the fact. The moment she managed to chase away one nagging, inchoate thought, three others swooped in to take its place. A surfeit of excitement, she supposed: everything was so new, so unfamiliar. Even the walk from the station to their lodgings, well under half a mile, had been filled with adventure.

The first thing to be seen upon disembarking was a series of billboards enclosing something like a circus, which a huge, illuminated sign identified as 'Uglieland'. From all appearances, the description was not inaccurate. A motley wall of bills and posters advertised everything from poker games to foreign dance orchestras and performing animals. In dawn's crisp light, the muddied shouts of revellers could still be heard from within. As Ana and her party passed by, a corrugated-iron gate swung open and a couple of sots were ejected, falling into the street in a gin-soaked heap. No sooner had she managed to negotiate the obstacle presented by these bedraggled figures than she was pulled unceremoniously to the side by Parkes, a crowded electric tram clattering through the space she had occupied only a moment earlier.

The morning wore on. More people crowded the shopfronts along Market Street than Ana had seen in the last decade, spilling out into the street, laughing and haggling. She heard deals being conducted in languages she could only guess at, saw stores that specialised in strange machinery, unfamiliar foods and foreign fashions. Women wore suit-like jackets or straight-lined dresses paired with coquettish caps; men went about bareheaded. And the bathing costumes! Bold and brazen, they stood in the shop windows, striped and spotted and all the more appealing for the scent of the sea drifting up from the beach at the bottom of High Street.

It was this, of course, that Ana would have most liked to investigate, but the detective sergeant was quick to curtail their flights of fancy. The minute their rooms were ready, he issued strict instructions for Ana and the mendicant to stay within. It would be a good opportunity, he said, to catch up on missed sleep, adding in a martyred tone that such a luxury was denied him. Instead, he was to head directly to the offices of J.H. Sweetingham & Company, nestled amongst the importers and conveyancers in the narrow streets of the town's west end. There he planned to lie in wait, as his quarry was expected at any moment—Arthur Beynon, or his killer, or some phantom that wore his face.

There, in all honesty, was the real reason that Ana had not managed a wink of sleep. The dead man. She could try to place the blame on the excitement of the city or the steadily strengthening sunlight, but the truth was that any time her eyes closed, the wretch's mangled face was waiting, and so was his killer, a formless shadow.

Parkes had been gone for several hours now, a silent and sullen Cooper in tow, and Ana was acutely aware that each passing minute brought the culprit closer. Closer to Fremantle, closer to her—and then what? Her thoughts began once more to buzz. Would she have to meet him? To speak to him? Surely, he could be identified from a distance, whoever he was—someone who shared his victim's face, somehow, and wore his name.

Suddenly, the room was too hot.

Ana kicked the bedclothes loose and struggled free. Hunched over the edge of the bed, she gulped a few fevered breaths. She wrenched off her nightdress and sat for a moment in underclothes alone, letting the heat evaporate from her sweat-sheened skin.

Several minutes later, her heart rate having returned to a semblance of normality, she opened her small travelling case, found her lightest frock and pulled it on. Out of the room she went, and into the narrow hallway, her bare feet sending motes of dust dancing from the thick, faded carpet to twirl in the light from a low window. She padded to the bathroom, which was large and relatively clean: no little luxury after days of travel.

A green patina had roughened the brass taps slightly, and they creaked in protest as she spun them open. With a strangled little sound from somewhere far below, the water began to flow. Ana caught it in cupped hands and splashed it over her face, gasping at the sudden coolness.

She looked at the woman in the tarnished mirror, hidden here and there by spots of damaged silver. Who was she, her dark curls dust-reddened and dripping? A stranger, or just someone older, someone stronger?

Slowly, her heart regained its usual rhythm. She reached for the soap.

* * *

The friar was on the first-floor balcony, one hand on the railing. At the sound of footsteps, he turned. It was Ana, sleepless but freshly scrubbed.

'I see I'm not alone in pacing my cage,' he smiled, before turning back to the view. 'As cages go, of course, I can think of far worse.'

The balcony faced north over High Street. The sea of humanity flowed beneath the watchers' feet, the creaking of cartwheels and snatches of children's chatter reaching up to envelope them. Beyond this, seen through the gaps in the buildings opposite, lay the harbour, forested with masts and rigging, the flags and funnels of steamers shifting almost imperceptibly with the whims of the tide. A cacophony of gulls hung over the port, swept aloft on the heat rising from wide summer streets. The vista was wide and warm, but Ana could not stifle a shiver. Somewhere out there was the killer.

'Do you think they'll catch him?' she wondered. 'It certainly wouldn't be hard for a fugitive to slip on board one of those ships.'

The friar thought for a moment, then shook his head. 'He tried to cover his tracks,' he said. 'That man—Arthur Beynon, or whoever he really is—could simply have run, but he took the time to hide the body, to make it seem as though nothing was wrong. That was an immense risk. He must have something worth protecting. A position, perhaps, or a family.'

'So he'll simply stroll into his office?' asked Ana. 'Just as if nothing had happened?'

'I don't see many other options open to him. I doubt he's even aware that his victim's body has been found.'

Ana took a moment to look at her companion. The sun was full on his face now, shadowing the furrowed lines of his brow and cheeks. She noticed for the first time that his hair was thinning in places, a smooth scalp peeking through the curls.

'You know something, don't you?' she said, suddenly. 'You know something about all this that I don't.'

'I suppose I do,' he smiled. 'Just as you know something that you haven't told me.'

A long, silent moment passed between them. On the street below, a paperboy cried his wares.

'Do you recall,' said the friar, rather abruptly, 'the name of the company for which our Mr Beynon works?'

Ana frowned, casting her mind back up the coast.

'J.H. Something-or-other,' she ventured.

The friar's face lit up with a grin. 'Yes,' he beamed. 'J.H. Sweetingham, I believe, though it's the "H" that leaps out at me. Not "H", mind you, but "*H*".'

To Ana, with the benefit of audible communication, this statement was more illuminating than it appears on the page. The friar was leaning heavily on the breathy sound at the beginning of the word, differentiating 'haitch' from 'aitch'. The theme was clearly a source of some excitement to him.

'It's what we call a "shibboleth", you see,' he went on. 'The word is taken from —'

'The Book of Judges,' interrupted Ana. 'The people of Gilead used it as a code word to flush out fugitive Ephraimites, who pronounced the "s" differently. You can save yourself the effort of explaining scripture to me.'

The friar flushed. 'Forgive me,' he said. 'I still slip rather too easily into sermon. I certainly didn't mean to imply that your own scholarship was insufficient.' Receiving Ana's absolution, he went on. 'In this case, though, the pronunciation differed not between two tribes, but between two renditions of the same man's words.'

In a moment, Ana understood.

'Cooper and the shopkeeper in Port Denison,' she said, with dawning excitement. 'They both sang Beynon's advertising jingle!'

'Exactly—and while Cooper used aitch, the proprietress used haitch.'

'How does that help us, though?' asked Ana. 'Neither pronunciation is particularly uncommon.'

'This is true,' the friar conceded, 'which is why I had the proprietress dictate the word "Wyndham" to me. She spelt it with an aitch, revealing that she uses haitch only when impersonating Arthur Beynon. What does that suggest?'

'Well, that Beynon uses haitch, of course.' Ana pulled herself up short, eyes wide. 'Except Cooper's version of him didn't.'

'Precisely. It's dangerous, of course, to operate upon assumptions,' came the friar's caveat, 'but Beynon has left us with a dearth of information and little choice. I'm assuming, therefore, that Cooper's obvious talent for impressions will render an accurate pronunciation. I am also assuming that the proprietress would not oscillate arbitrarily between two ways of pronouncing the same letter. If she used haitch, it is only because her subject did so.'

Ana nodded impatiently.

'My final assumption, then,' the friar went on, 'is that Arthur Beynon would also naturally favour one pronunciation over the other, not flipping back and forth. The fact that two of his acquaintances reported his jingle differently, therefore, presents very few logical possibilities.'

Ana's impatience had, by now, reached a dangerous level.

'What possibilities?' she asked, each syllable a staccato stab.

'Well, Cooper met the man a year ago. It's possible that since that time, some strange circumstance has caused Beynon to alter his pronunciation of a single letter, while his appearance, demeanour and the rest of his sales patter remained unchanged. An example of such a circumstance, I must admit, does not spring readily to mind.'

Ana's eyebrows gave indication that she, too, was unimpressed by this scenario. The friar decided to skip the less convincing options and cut directly to his primary hypothesis.

'There is one configuration of possibilities which, although thoroughly singular, does fit with all the facts. We have been operating under the idea that the man who died was Arthur Beynon, and that the man who killed him has assumed his identity somehow, most likely in the hopes of eluding capture or suspicion.' He drummed his fingers on the wrought-iron handrail. 'It is possible—very improbable, I'll admit, but the truth often is—that the Arthur Beynon encountered by Cooper and the Arthur Beynon who services Port Denison are not the same man, and that they never were the same man.'

For a minute or two, Ana turned the idea over.

Her first instinct had been to laugh—it was, as the mendicant admitted, thoroughly unlikely—but at the same time, there was no hard and fast reason that it *couldn't* be true. Indeed, if two men were to share the same identity, the peculiar set of conditions created by the distance and adversity of Australia's north-west would be quite conducive to the caper, in a way. The most immediate and obvious opposition to the idea, though, remained that of motivation.

'Why on earth would two people pretend to be one?' said Ana. 'And if, for whatever reason, someone did go to all the effort of assuming another man's identity—with his knowledge and cooperation, of course, or the whole idea *would* be impossible—then why would he choose a travelling lamp salesman?'

'That's what baffles me, I'm afraid. Now it can baffle you, too,' the friar laughed, 'until such time as we finally have him.'

There was a heavy step upon the balcony and they turned to see the detective sergeant emerge from the corridor. A broad grin shook the tips of his moustache.

'We finally have him,' he said.

CHAPTER FOURTEEN

They waited in the library. It was a room which seemed to have earned its name merely by having a greater number of books than any other in the hotel, much as a duellist whose opponent is struck by lightning might be deemed the victor.

Brushing dust from the room's single shelf, Ana scanned the collection, hoping to find a gem secreted amongst its scant offerings. Of course, even if she were to unearth something thrilling hidden away between the tattered field manual on agricultural drainage and the three remaining volumes of what had once been a thirty-six part encyclopedia, she would never have been able to sit still long enough to make it past the first page. She and the friar had occupied the room for less than a quarter of an hour, but the tension wrought havoc on time, wringing eternities from every second.

The detective sergeant's instructions had been very clear. They were to go immediately to the library and wait there until preparations for the interview had been completed and the prisoner brought in. His reasons for electing to transform the space into an ad hoc interrogation room were esoteric at best, particularly as the Fremantle police station was close enough to be glimpsed from the balcony, but Ana suspected it had something to do with the detective sergeant's desire to mitigate the inevitable bureaucracy of a crime which fell under more than one jurisdiction.

This supposition, while certainly not wrong, failed to strike at Parkes's primary motivation, which was pride. The man in his custody had baffled him for three hundred miles, and now that he finally had the fellow, no soft city constable was going to share his triumph.

Ana paced the room once more, drawing creaks of complaint from the floorboards. The friar was frustratingly silent. Immediately upon entering, he had sunk into an old armchair and closed his eyes. He sat there still, lips moving slightly in some musing or meditation. Had Ana been ignorant of his apostasy, she might have thought it a prayer.

When the door finally opened, so too did the mendicant's eyes. Ana whipped round, breathless, but it was only one of the hotel's messenger-boys bearing a pitcher of water and a tea set on a silver tray. Smiling apologetically in the face of his guests' obvious disappointment, he arranged the cups and glasses on a small side-table, each china clink deafening in the expectant air.

The boy returned time and again in the following minutes, bringing a stack of papers and a decanter of some dark liquor, among other minutiae. So accustomed did Ana become to these quotidian intrusions that when, at last, the accused was led into the room, she didn't so much as look up from the bookshelf.

Then, in a moment, he was in front of her.

With Cooper and Parkes on either arm, the man was ushered unceremoniously into a faded rocking chair in the corner of the room. The defiant set of his jaw was undermined somewhat both by the chair's slow back-and-forth bob and the obvious anxiety in his wide green eyes, which flickered about the room. They passed over Ana without the slightest hint of recognition.

She knew him, though—or, at the very least, she thought she did. If it hadn't been for the half-stripped face in the soil at Wongoondy, and all this talk of two men with the same name, she would have been certain, but in the light of everything that had happened, she forced herself to take a second look. And then a third.

He certainly looked like the man she had found bleeding by the rock. She struggled to call the particulars to mind. Though less than a week ago, details of the night swam like a childhood nightmare. The clothes were the same, definitely, and that tawny beard could easily have been the one she saw grow stiff and heavy with blood. She fought to suppress a shudder. The hair, too, was the same: not too short, slightly wavy and clinging to the forehead. Beneath it, though, those brows—were they thicker than she remembered? Was the nose a little smaller? It was impossible to be sure.

For a few moments, the only sound was the slowing creak of the rocking chair. Then, for the first time since entering the room, the detective sergeant spoke.

'Please be so good as to tell us your name,' he said, quietly.

Ana leaned unwittingly forward, steadying herself against the shelf with a trembling hand, trying to glean something— anything—from the man's response.

'I've already told you my name,' was all he said.

Whereas the detective sergeant's speech bore the broad accents of his antipodean upbringing, and Ana's adoptive parents broadcast their Liverpudlian origins with every word, the man in the rocking chair gave nothing away. His voice was quiet and controlled, with not a trace of feeling.

'You've told me,' said Parkes. 'I'd like you to tell my associates.'

The man in the rocking chair glanced around his audience, as if trying to discern what strange purpose could have made comrades of so disparate a group. Parkes stood before him, arms folded. Ana was half-hidden by the dusty bookshelf, while the mendicant sat barefoot and cross-legged on one end of a long leather sofa, having shed his sandals. Cooper had retreated to the entrance, where he stood with one leg propped against the doorframe, hat pulled low over his face. There were no windows in the library. A single electric globe hung from the high ceiling, throwing shadows across the walls.

'My name,' said the man in the rocking chair, 'is Arthur Beynon.'

Unable to ignore the subtle, silent thrill this revelation sent through the library, he turned to Parkes.

'I think you'll agree that I've been most obliging. Perhaps you'll do me the same courtesy and tell me why you've brought me here. I'm not under suspicion of anything, surely?'

The detective sergeant ignored the question. 'We have not yet completed the introductions,' he chided, blithely calm. 'But wait—I'd nearly forgotten! Of course, you already know my good colleague, Mr Cooper. You met him, as I'm sure you'll remember, not far from Mount Magnet.'

Parkes delivered this short soliloquy without once breaking eye contact. He saw the sudden panic agitate his quarry's features, the supreme effort exerted to bring them back under control. He saw, too, the practised stagecraft that went into the man's subsequent transformation. With a wide, sudden grin, the accused leapt up from his rocking chair, clapping a hand to his forehead.

'Cooper! That was it. You must forgive me, old man,' he laughed heartily. 'I knew I recognised you, but truth be told, I'm no good with names. Head like a sieve, you know—and, of course, one meets so many people in this line of work, it can be hard to keep them all straight.' He held out a hand. 'An absolute pleasure to run into you again.'

It was a praiseworthy performance, and could almost have been sufficient to allay suspicion, were it not for a single, crucial miscalculation: the man who wasn't Arthur Beynon was addressing a man who wasn't Cooper. His outstretched hand hung absurdly in front of the friar. The mendicant's sympathetic little smile alerted him to his mistake—and all its implications—a moment too late, and he sank back into his seat. The rocking chair creaked plaintively, an absurd, punitive coda.

Parkes laughed. 'This is Cooper,' he said, stomping over to clap the tracker on the shoulder. 'And *this*,' he bent to the pile of papers on the side-table, 'is Arthur Beynon.'

Madeleine Dawson's sketch was held aloft for all eyes to see.

'It would appear you're better with faces than with names,' the detective sergeant went on. 'You certainly did a hell of a job stealing this one.'

He tossed the sketch into the man's lap.

'What I'd like to know, though, is *why*. Why kill Beynon? Why go to all this trouble to impersonate a lamp salesman, of all people?'

Parkes was evidently not alone in wanting to know this, as the room grew close with ill-concealed anticipation.

The man in the rocking chair did not immediately respond. He held the portrait with both hands, gazing intently at the face of his doppelgänger. To Ana, it seemed as though he was about to cry. When he did finally find his voice again, it was a little thicker, a little softer.

'I didn't kill Arthur,' he said, 'and you'll have an awful lot of difficulty trying to prove that I did.'

He spoke with a sort of sad certainty, his tone neither stubborn nor confrontational. 'My papers are in order and I can name any number of witnesses who will readily testify to the fact that I am Arthur Beynon.'

The detective sergeant's face coloured swiftly, his fists tightening. The suspect's thorough lack of feeling was more infuriating, somehow, than any brazen gloating.

'I'm not sure that's an entirely accurate assessment of the situation.'

Four heads turned as one. It was the friar who had spoken. He was still in the same position on the leather lounge, legs crossed beneath his cassock, but sat straighter now, keen and alert. He smiled.

'You seem to be unaware that there was a witness present at the moment of death. A witness who is presently among us.'

Parkes turned on the friar, his cheeks now a deep, apoplectic red. Before he could reprimand the little man for speaking out of turn, however, he caught sight of the suspect's face. It was alive with hope. The mendicant had seen it too. Seizing the moment, he leapt to his feet.

'I thought as much!' he said. 'You didn't kill him—but you'd like to know who did.' With a quick, fluid movement, he dropped to his knees in front of the rocking chair, staring up into the suspect's eyes. 'We can help you find him. Beynon was dear to you, wasn't he?'

For a long moment, the man in the chair said nothing. A single, slow tear rolled down his roughened cheek and was lost amongst his whiskers. Then, the levee broken, he dissolved into a fit of heaving sobs.

The detective sergeant writhed in discomfort. Having his interrogation hijacked was bad enough without this sudden and unseemly display of emotion. His immediate instinct was to shout down the lot of them and wrest control back from the friar. In an almost superhuman display of self-control, however, he forced himself to stay silent. Though undeniably stubborn, Parkes was not stupid, and it was plain to see that the mendicant was making some sort of progress, however obscure his methods. With a sigh, he made his way back to the side-table and lifted the decanter, pouring himself a generous tumblerful of whiskey.

This admirable show of restraint was almost undone altogether when the friar appeared at his side and, with a little murmur of thanks, relieved him of the drink, taking it over to the man in the rocking chair. Stifling the urge to arrest everyone in the room on charges of perverting the course of justice, Parkes soon managed to calm himself sufficiently to pour a second tumbler. Nursing it, he retreated to the sofa to watch.

'Why don't you tell us what you know?' suggested the mendicant.

The man in the rocking chair hesitated, knuckles white around his glass. His cheeks still glistened.

'You wouldn't believe me,' he said. 'It's a long story, and quite incredible.'

'In my experience,' countered the friar, 'it's the incredible accounts which are most often true. Liars tend to keep their stories neat. Reality, on the other hand, is inherently untidy.'

The suspect's lips twitched in the beginnings of a smile, but he still seemed reluctant to speak.

The friar reached out to take Madeleine's portrait, studying it for a few careful seconds.

'Do you have any idea who might have wanted to kill Arthur Beynon?' he asked.

To the surprise of everyone else in the room, the man in the rocking chair gave a little laugh.

'Who wouldn't? He was a liar and a cheat. A thorough bastard till the end.' He lifted his glass towards the sketch. 'That's not Arthur Beynon, though. Arthur Beynon has been dead for a decade.'

CHAPTER FIFTEEN

'My name is Cyril,' said the man in the rocking chair. 'Cyril Brennan. I was born in Dun Laoghaire, two years before the turn of the century.' At this, the onlookers resumed their seats, and Cooper made his way quietly over to an armchair. If the man's story began in the reign of Queen Victoria, they were going to be listening for a while.

'There were four of us kids, all told,' Cyril went on. 'Two sisters, my brother and myself. Ma worked at the schoolhouse and my father laid bricks for a living—really, though, he was a Fenian. That's what took most of his time—the fight for a free Ireland.'

Notes of the man's original accent crept into his speech as he sank further into memory, but the changes were slow and subtle. It had clearly been a long time since he had broken character.

'We were happy enough, I suppose,' he said. 'Neither rich nor poor. Nothing much happening in our house. The old man kept himself clean, for the most part. Some people whispered that he'd had something to do with the Phoenix Park trouble— long before my time, that was—but mostly he was just printing leaflets and handing them out at rallies. He was kind to us; proud of us all, he always said. Good to Ma, too, though that's not saying much—you'd be hard-pressed to find a soul that could speak a word in anger to Ma Brennan.' He smiled into his glass, face warm with distant memory. 'Even when the war came, we weren't too worried at first. If the English were busy on the continent, so much the better for us. That's the way a lot of people thought, at the beginning. Plenty of outright support for the Germans, too. Some people were going so far as to say we should help 'em out, stop the Brits from harassing us for good. Towards the end of nineteen fourteen, though, the reports from the front started to reach us. Eventually, my father changed his tune, too; he knew the Kaiser was serious. If Britain falls, he said, what'll stop the Germans coming for us? So I joined up.'

He readjusted his legs a little, causing the chair to quietly rock. 'I had to lie about my age. I was just a few months over my sixteenth birthday. Sean wanted to enlist, too—my brother, that is—but he was nearly two years younger and couldn't quite manage the beard I could, so he was there at the quay with Ma and the girls, waving me off. Father stayed home. They wouldn't take him for the army because he'd had consumption, and he said he couldn't take the shame of standing with a crowd of women and children as the men went off to war. I watched them all grow small as the ship slipped away till I couldn't make out which one was Ma. I stood at the stern, with two dozen others, all under twenty. Each of us thought we were the only one trying not to cry. We were off to join the Royal Irish Regiment.'

Cyril raised the glass to his lips for a moment. The others waited, now utterly silent.

'I had no idea how long I'd be gone. None of us knew the war would last four years, of course. How could we? I got lucky, though. I was at La Bassée for only two months.'

He pulled aside the loose collar of his shirt to reveal a dark, twisted scar below his left collarbone.

'I took a bayonet to the shoulder,' he said. 'After stitching me up, they sent me north to help with the supply lines.' He smiled. 'Invalid work. I was more or less out of the line of fire for the next year. In fact, it wasn't the Germans that finally put an end to my military career—it was pneumonia. I was sent back to the military hospital at Clonmel to recover. It was strange, after all that time, to be so close to home. Only a hundred miles from Dublin; my family could have made the journey in a day! Unfortunately, visitors were not permitted, and even if they had been, I was in no state to receive anyone. For months, I drifted in and out of consciousness. There were three or four occasions when I was positive that I was dying. Slowly, though, week by week, month by month, I recovered. I was allowed out of bed for an hour a day, then longer. Soon, I was taking walks in the hospital grounds, and then, at long last, I was given the all-clear to return to service. They didn't send me straight back to the front, though. They allocated me to the reserves, the third battalion. This was nineteen sixteen. The week before Easter.'

Ana knew little of the war and less of Ireland, but she saw both Parkes and the friar stiffen as the implication of the date sank in.

'What is it?' she asked. 'What happened?'

Brennan looked up in surprise; it was the first time he had heard the young woman speak.

'The Easter Rising,' said Parkes. 'A rebellion. A group of nationalists tried to take advantage of the war on the continent to force the British out of Ireland.'

Brennan nodded. 'A thousand-odd armed insurrectionists on the streets of Dublin,' he said. 'My father, of course, among them. And who do you suppose they sent in to try and put them down?' He gave a sad little chuckle. 'Put yourself in my place. I was loyal, of course, to the men I fought with at the front. Many of them gave their lives for me, and I would have done the same for them. Still, I loved my homeland—I'd signed up to protect it, after all—and had seen it suffer under indifferent British administration for far too long. What was I to do? What *could* I do? Defect to fight with the Fenians and risk being court-martialled and executed for treason? Fire on my own people, betraying my father and my ideals?'

He looked at each member of his audience in turn, as if still hoping for a solution.

'What did you do?' asked Ana.

'I ran,' said Brennan, simply. 'I fled. You may call it cowardly— perhaps it was—but I could see no other option. Our troop was sent into the city on the back of a covered truck. As soon as it began to slow down, I leapt off, shouting that I'd seen a saboteur running down a side street. The moment my comrades were out of sight, I leapt over a low wall into what turned out to be a boarding school. Luckily, the holy week meant that it was all but empty. I stripped to my undershirt and long-johns, throwing my weapons and my uniform into a rosebush, and broke into the building through a low window. I spent nearly an hour rifling through the deserted dormitories, looking for the rooms of the senior boys in the hope that some clothes my size might have been left behind. I finally found a jacket and some old riding trousers; they were a little too small and made me look quite ridiculous, but at least I was no longer identifiable as a soldier. I slipped back out onto the streets as a civilian, managing to steer clear of most of the fighting.'

'Where did you go?' pressed Ana, completely failing to disguise her enjoyment of the man's escapades.

'I wanted to go home,' said Brennan, 'but I knew that it was no longer an option. The only thing I could think of was to get away completely, to go where I wouldn't be recognised by either side. I went east, heading for the docks. I stuck to the alleys and the backstreets, doubling back whenever I heard gunfire. Even so, it wasn't long before I ran into a group of rebels; seeing that I was unarmed, though, they let me pass. After that, my luck held, and I made it to the water almost unnoticed—or so I thought.'

Here, he paused to take a drink, unaware of the dangerous level of narrative tension to which he was subjecting Ana.

'There was no shortage of ships setting out. I doubt they had all planned to leave that morning, but the pitched battles in the street must have made imminent departure seem like an expedient idea, under the circumstances. There were crowds of people pushing to get on to the gangways. Some of them, I assume, must have been passengers or crew, but most seemed, like me, to be simply seeking a way out. I had no ticket and no money, but in the commotion, it wasn't hard to slip through the throng and lose myself aboard a crowded vessel. I didn't know where it was heading, and I didn't much care; my only thought was escape. It wasn't until we were well and truly out to sea that I realised I had been followed.'

'By whom?' asked Ana, clutching at her locket.

'By Sean. I'd hidden myself in the hold, finally thinking that I might have gotten away with it all, when I felt a tap on my shoulder. I spun around, and there he was. My little brother. I was overjoyed, of course; it was the first time we had seen each other in nearly two years. It so happened that he had been running reconnaissance for the rebels and had seen me darting through an alley. He thought his eyes must've been playing tricks on him, so he followed me to the docks, and there we both ended up. In the hold of a ship heading God-knows-where.' He sighed. 'I won't bore you too much with our travels from that point forward. We soon found out, of course, that returning to Ireland was impossible. Within days, the British had quelled the rebellion and were summarily executing those involved, which meant that Sean would never be safe at home. As a deserter from the British army, my position was far worse; half of Europe was off limits. We skulked from port to port, living like rats, stowing away on ships and hiding in warehouses. It was a filthy, feral life. We were sickly and starving, more often than not. I don't think we would have lasted much longer had we not been discovered. It was a day or so out of Bristol, on a supply ship bound for Cape Town. We had made ourselves a crude bed in a crate of bully beef, deep in the hold. The odds of being discovered, we thought, were fairly low. After all, what kind of creature would creep through the belly of a supply ship and pry open containers of supplies for fun?' Brennan gave a bitter laugh. 'Arthur Beynon!' he said. 'That's who. He wasn't a stowaway, though—his father had paid for his passage, and plenty more besides. They were a wealthy family from Birmingham. Owned a few factories, I believe. It seems that young Arthur, far from being ready to assume the mantle of responsibility, had left a string of heartbroken young women across the Midlands, at least one of whom was in the family way. After paying her to stay silent, the elder Beynon was looking for a way to get his son out from under his feet, at least for a few years, but couldn't risk having his line snuffed out in the trenches by a stray bullet. As luck would have it, there was an old family friend who had made quite something of himself in the colonies, opening a saddlery or something in Melbourne before expanding into Sydney and Adelaide. Young Arthur was to work with him awhile, learn the ropes, keep his head down. Once the war had petered out and things had settled on the domestic front, the scion could return to take his rightful place at the helm of the family business and all would be right with the world. Less than twenty-four hours out of his father's sight, though, Arthur had already tired of life on the straight and narrow. He was on the lookout for a plaything, something to pass the time. He found us.'

Here, the narrator paused to drain his glass. Ana hastened to refill it. She was clearly transported, hanging on the Irishman's every word. The others, though receptive, appeared more reserved.

The little friar wore an attentive smile, but this was the norm, rather than an exception. The detective sergeant sat stiffly, arms folded against his chest; he seemed to be following the story closely, but without sympathy. Cooper was silent and inscrutable, eyes fixed for the most part on the faded rug in the centre of the room. Whenever Brennan paused, though, the tracker would look up, as if prompting him to continue. Buoyed by this, and the fresh tumbler of whiskey that Ana pushed into his hand, the Irishman pressed onwards.

'At first, Arthur was thoroughly charming. He brought us titbits from the galley, played cards with us, swapped stories. It seemed, however, that kindness could only hold his interest for so long. He soon realised that he had two men thoroughly at his mercy. A word from him to the captain and we would be discovered, cast adrift or thrown into prison at the next port. We had nothing of value to offer him. Nothing, that is, but our pride. In the deepest corners of the hold, he'd force Sean and I to box, race or wrestle for his amusement. When he tired of competition, he had us eat the weevils that crawled amongst the cases of ship's biscuit, or the roaches that scuttled along in the dark. He'd taunt us with the lives that lay in wait for us. At Cape Town, he smuggled us on to the next ship, concealed in his luggage. We were bound for Fremantle now, and he made it clear that there was no freedom to be had in Australia, either. We would follow him to Victoria and pose as his loyal servants. Working without pay, we were to play an instrumental role in his ambitions. He planned to wrest control of the business from his father's friend, having first won his trust. He talked like this for hours, often working himself into such a frenzy that I worried we would be discovered. The ultimate goal, it seemed, was always to leave his father furious and destitute. He was a vain, petty man, and I hated him.'

Brennan looked from the friar to Parkes. 'I shouldn't tell you this. I know how precarious my position is, how far-fetched this all sounds. I won't lie to you, though. I wanted to kill Arthur Beynon. I longed for it. Sean and I spent whole nights scheming, in the dark, heaving waters beyond the Cape of Good Hope. We dreamed of throwing him into the sea during a storm or gagging him and sealing him inside a crate. Our ship was bound first for Singapore, so we had plenty of time to plan. Who knows? If the right opportunity had arisen, I might now have the weight of a man's murder on my conscience. As it was, though, the Abrolhos took that weight from me.'

Here, for the first time, the mendicant interjected. 'The Abrolhos?' he queried.

'An island chain,' said Ana, failing to hide the impatience in her voice. 'It's about fifty miles west of Geraldton.'

'Lot of crayfish,' added Cooper. 'Lot of shipwrecks.'

'The latter's what got us,' said Brennan. 'It was nearly midnight when we passed the islands, though Sean and I didn't know that, of course. Day and night were one and the same to us, down in the hold. We heard a tremendous noise and knew immediately that we'd hit something. The ship lurched at an awkward angle, and there were cries from above. We waited for a good while, unsure whether to risk showing ourselves. Then we heard the water rushing in and realised we no longer had a choice. We crept up to the deck—it was chaos. The passengers and crew were in the midst of evacuating. We knew that the situation must be dire, as no-one had bothered to try salvaging anything from the hold; they simply grabbed whatever was to hand and leapt for the lifeboats. We did the same, and just in time, making it on to the second last boat. In all the commotion, it was a minute or two before anyone noticed that we were newcomers. Even then, they were in no situation to do anything about it. We had to get clear of the ship, you see, and the sea was rough as anything. There were twelve of us in the boat—including, as luck would have it, Arthur Beynon—and there must have been four or five other boats besides, but as the storm festered and the waves grew higher, we lost sight of them, one by one. It was a biblical upheaval. Sudden mountains of water were thrown up, lifting us high into the writhing sky; then, just as quickly, they'd drop us, and the whole world seemed to tilt and fall away. For awful, endless moments, we hung in the air.'

Brennan's whiskey glass played the role of the lifeboat in his enthusiastic re-enactment, sending rivulets of the dark liquor flying. 'Then, inevitably, the crash.' He brought the glass heavily down into his lap, heedless of the spray. 'I don't know how many times it happened, but I can tell you that, in the end, it was one time too many. With a slow, awful creak, the timbers caved in. It was as if they'd simply given up, folding away from the boat's spine. We fell into the black water, all mixed up together in one squealing mass, like a bag of kittens thrown into a well. We clung to shattered timbers, to each other, to anything that showed signs of being able to float. I'm not much of a swimmer, I'll freely confess, and neither is Sean—our old man often boasted of being able to swim the width of Lough Tay, but I'll bet it was all bluster. One by one, we lost sight of the others. They were taken by sudden heaving swells, or simply succumbed to cramps in the frigid water and slipped silently beneath the waves. I didn't see Beynon disappear. He was simply there one minute and gone the next. What happened to the other boats, I've no idea, but I do know that they never reached shore. I read the reports in the *West Australian*, weeks later, and they all said the same thing—no survivors.'

'Of course!' the detective sergeant snapped his fingers. 'The *Enlightenment*. That was the ship, wasn't it? About ten years back?'

Cyril Brennan nodded. 'June, nineteen seventeen,' he said. 'Collided with a reef and was lost with all hands. Well, all hands on the register, at least. Sean and I held fast to our flotsam. At last, the sky began to grow light, and for a brief and blissful moment, the sun breathed life back into us. I felt my frozen fingers thaw, the lead weight of my legs grow just a little lighter. After shivering the whole night through, I was finally still, or as still as the waves would allow. Unfortunately, the respite was over in an hour—two at the most. Soon enough, the peace brought by the warming dawn evaporated. The sun grew hotter and higher. By noon, we were cooked like crabs, red and shining in the shadowless sea. The glare was intolerable; my brother's burnt face swam before me, squinting and salt-rimed. And so it went on. We froze through three long nights, praying for the sun to save us, then cursed every second of the searing light that followed. On the afternoon of the third day, I noticed that Sean was still shivering, even as he burned. A fever had set in, though for some inexplicable reason, I was spared.'

He glared around the room, clearly suffering from the combined assault of memory and alcohol. His glass was empty now, the whiskey lengthening his vowels and loosening his gestures. 'I began to scream at the sky. Shouted myself hoarse. I was thoroughly convinced that fate was having its fickle way with me, toying with me like a cat plays with a mouse, or a blackfish knocks a seal pup around an icefloe. Sent to war, banished from my homeland, now lost in some sodden purgatory, watching my brother cough himself to death. Why go on? I bellowed at the waves but received no reply. Sean was weakening; between bringing up blood, he began to speak of letting go, giving up, letting the sea take him. I was almost ready to join him, especially as I saw the flies begin to find his fissured lips. I was worried that he would waste the little strength he had left in swatting them away, but he simply burst into laughter. This, as you can imagine, did little to soothe me—I thought the suffering had finally robbed him of his wits. It wasn't the laughter of madness, though, but pure joy. Fatigued as I was, it took me an age to cotton on, but the second I realised, I was laughing right beside him.'

An echo of that ancient mirth danced in Cyril's eyes now.

'Flies won't survive at sea, of course,' he grinned. 'Just like us, they need land. I craned my aching neck around, and there it was; a russet stretch of godsent beach, reaching out to infinity at either end. Just like that,' he snapped his fingers, 'my luck was back in. I was glad enough of the land, of course—a lifetime of miracles, I thought, all at once—but it didn't stop there. When we'd finally managed to drag ourselves clear of the sea, we got our first good look at what it was we'd been clinging to.'

'Arthur Beynon's trunk,' said the friar.

The others turned as one.

'Incredible!' Cyril blinked back his shock. 'I mean, you're absolutely right, but—but how could you know?'

The friar gave an insouciant little shrug, attempting to appear modest and failing quite remarkably. 'Because it fits,' he said, simply. 'You said earlier that your papers were in order. I suppose it was finding the trunk that gave you the idea in the first place. Australia may no longer be a British colony, but the links between the two nations are still strong enough, and it wouldn't do to go about wearing a traitor's name, especially before the war had fully run its course. Life would be much easier as Arthur Beynon—you'd have a passport and legitimate immigration documents, to begin with—and provided you stayed on the west coast, there'd be little chance of running into anyone who knew the real Beynon.'

'You're quite correct, but I'm afraid you overestimate me,' said Cyril. 'The possibilities should have been clear from the moment I got the trunk open, but I was in no fit state to grasp them. My brother, you must remember, was gravely ill, and the first order of business was to get him some help. It wasn't easy. We were still well aware of the need to steer clear of the authorities, so I had to leave Sean hidden in the dunes while I went searching for aid. I had a few close calls, but my run of luck held, and I soon found a sympathetic fisherman who offered to take us to a place he knew. It was a huge sort of farm—or station, as I soon learned to call it—where questions would not be asked.' He smiled. 'It's strange, I suppose, to feel so safe amongst people who are almost certainly criminals, but that place became a refuge for us. There was a sort of camaraderie brought on by our shared burden, by the fear of being found out. The work was hard, but there was food and drink enough to keep us going. More importantly, after all those months in a crate at sea, there was solid ground, clean air and sunshine. It was paradise. They even had a fellow who came through to treat livestock ailments. He'd been a pharmacist, I think, but had his certification scrapped for some indiscretion which he didn't see fit to disclose. He dosed Sean with a serum meant for cattle. I thought it'd be the final nail in my brother's coffin, but miraculously, it seemed to help. Within a week, his fever was gone and the coughing had stopped, though it was months before he was strong enough to work. Unfortunately, that proved to be a problem. While the jackaroos and station hands were flush with solidarity, the boss himself was determined not to run a charity. I had my room and board, and I worked for it, but if Sean was to keep storing himself and his swag in the big shearing shed, he'd have to pay.'

Cyril turned to the mendicant. 'It was only then that I finally began to inspect the contents of the trunk in earnest,' he said. 'That's when the plan started to come together. Beynon had amassed plenty of trinkets, some good books and a sturdy coat; they bought a bed and food for the length of Sean's convalescence. I kept Beynon's watch, the rest of his clothing and personal effects. Most importantly, of course, I kept his papers. Armed with my new name, I went out to find a job that could support us both. Something that would give us the opportunity to be comfortable, not just to survive. We wanted to get back to Ireland eventually, of course, but we still had no idea how long the war would last, or what might come after. My initial thought was to set myself up in some respectable business which would allow me to hire Sean under an assumed identity. I had to protect him, you see. I had to. He was my little brother.'

These last few words slipped out in a desperate little whisper. Cyril took a moment to compose himself before continuing.

'I went south. Through Geraldton, first, then on down through the wheatbelt to Perth and Fremantle. Despite the war, there was work enough to be had, and I spoke with no fewer than a dozen prospective employers. The more time I spent talking to people, though, the more I realised that an assumed name would never give Sean the life he deserved. Without the correct papers, he couldn't be admitted to hospital, couldn't book passage on a ship. He'd be a shadow. Half a man. And that,' said Cyril, with an odd, abrupt smile, 'is when the idea struck me. Could I live as half a man? Could anyone?' As if expecting an answer, he looked at each member of his audience in turn. 'I had taken possession of one man's legal identity,' he went on. 'Perhaps—just perhaps—it would be possible for Sean and myself to share it.'

A slow understanding spread through the room.

'You can imagine, then, the appeal of the job with Sweetingham and Company. It was ideal, really. There were easier jobs on offer, and higher-paying ones, too—in taking Beynon's name, I had also come into possession of letters of reference from Eton—but the humble lot of the travelling salesman suited me down to the ground. As the managing director sketched out the route on his wall map, from Fremantle up to Carnarvon, I saw exactly how it would all fit together. In a flash, I saw the whole thing before me.' A note of pride crept into his voice. 'It was quite simple, really. I took the route from Fremantle up to Geraldton and Sean took everything further north. We went up the coastal roads and back down through the goldfields. There wasn't a single person in the whole state who actually knew what Beynon looked like, so we didn't have to work hard at our disguises. Luckily, we've always looked alike—both take after our da—so it was mostly a matter of getting the beards and the clothing right. We made our changeovers at night, to avoid being spotted. We'd have to take a few hours, of course, to catch each other up on things. What we'd sold, who we'd spoken to, any significant events we'd been present for. That helped us to avoid most of the suspicion. Even if we did forget someone, though, it was fairly easy to blame it on the job. All those names and faces, all those miles—who could fault us?'

'Where did you stay?' asked Ana, propelled by a curiosity that far outpaced the narrative. 'You must have had to keep out of sight while Sean was up north. It wouldn't do for Beynon to be seen in two places at once.'

'Ah, you're a natural at this!' Cyril laughed. 'You're right, of course. I had to be in hiding while Sean was playing at being Beynon, just as he had to disappear when I took over. For the first few years, we'd switch off shifts at the station that took us in after the wreck. No questions asked, remember? Not only that, it also gave us a chance to earn a little extra money. Between those wages and the money from Sweetingham and Company, we were eventually able to purchase our own property—near Tenindewa, just west of Mullewa—and that became our safe house. We still visited the station regularly, though.' The smile stiffened a little, became grim. 'Old Lucas's place was a second home for us both. Right till the end.'

'Lucas?' the detective sergeant gave a start, as if jolted suddenly from sleep. 'I knew it!' He slammed his fist into a heavy palm. 'All along, I knew it! He had "crooked" written all over him. But that can only mean that the body was —' he stopped short.

'Sean.' Cyril sighed. 'Yes. I left him there in that God-awful bog, naked and lifeless and alone. It was the most unforgivable thing I've ever done. No fit grave even for a murderer. I was in a panic, though, and couldn't think. It was as if my brain had simply shut down. I needed to hide him, you see. My first instinct was to ask Lucas for help, but I know Lucas—he only keeps a matter hidden as long as it pays him to do so. I'd heard about the likes of you trackers, too,' he tossed a look at Cooper, 'and I couldn't risk someone unearthing Sean and identifying him as Beynon. Then I happened upon the pigsty. I'd seen those swine get to work on dead things before—sheep, cattle, you name it—and I knew they'd make short work of Sean. It was a hideous idea, but I couldn't lose everything—not again. See, we had a plan, Sean and me. After the war, things still weren't looking too rosy for Ireland. But in Western Australia—well, we had a house now, and land almost half the size of County Clare. Sean had even started digging for gold in the back paddocks whilst I was playing at being Beynon. We were going to write to our parents and the girls—our sisters, that is—and bring them out here to be with us.' Here, his voice wavered a little. 'We were going to be a family again.'

'Then why did you kill him?' asked Parkes, bluntly.

For a moment, it looked as though Cyril was about to strike the policeman; his eyes were wild, his hands tightened into fists.

'Kill him?' he cried. 'Have you been listening at all, man? He was my brother. My brother! You've heard all I've had to say, all we'd been through together—do I sound like a man who could kill his kin?'

Parkes had to concede that it was unlikely. 'Who did it, then?' he asked.

'That's what I'd like to know,' said Cyril, still simmering. 'Some coward clubbed him, out there in the bush. He was due back on Wednesday night. I waited the whole night through, and the following day, too. When he still didn't show, I slipped out of the house and went to trace his steps. I knew the routes he took, see, just as he knew mine—we'd been over them again and again. I found him just around midnight, a little way north of Mullewa. He'd been fetched an awful blow across the head and left there to die, though the Lord only knows why. They didn't take anything, not even the horse. I found her wandering a way off to the south, cart and all.'

There was a numb silence. Cyril looked about in supplication.

'So that's it, then?' he said. 'None of you can tell me any more than that?'

The detective sergeant mumbled a little, shamefaced, but it was the friar who finally spoke.

'Actually,' he said, softly. 'I think I may be able to shed some light on what happened to your brother.'

CHAPTER SIXTEEN

The friar's claim was quite extraordinary.

Every remaining mystery in the case at hand, he said, could be explained. Despite the twisting strands of the stories involved, the answers would be clear, concrete and demonstrable via logical progression. There was nothing supernatural at play, nothing more sinister than the usual dark things which lurk in the hearts of men. Inevitably, though, the claim came with a caveat, and one that undercut the immediate impact of his assertion quite significantly: he would need the rest of the afternoon to gather a few final pieces of evidence.

The detective sergeant's first thought was simply to forbid the whole thing, seeing it as a prank or a ploy for freedom, a particularly tasteless tilt at escape, perhaps, from a character he still regarded as suspicious.

The friar, however, protested his innocence.

'I'm more than willing to wager my reputation,' he said.

'A reputation,' said Parkes, 'is just the latest in a long line of things you appear to have mislaid. If I had to hazard a guess, I'd say you left it in the same place as your name, your money and your alibi.'

The mendicant took this jibe with a good-natured laugh.

'I think it's more likely to be somewhere among your papers,' he said, nodding at the small stack of correspondence which still sat on the side-table.

'What the hell are you playing at?' the detective sergeant growled, his voice thick with suspicion. He stomped over to the little pile of papers and began to flick through them one by one, tossing aside reports from his constables and other routine documents. Finally, he came upon an unknown envelope, addressed to him care of the Fremantle post office. He held it up to the light to reveal a Dongara postmark, which Ana recognised at once. It was the letter the friar had written in the little seaside store at Port Denison.

Parkes made a half-hearted attempt to preserve the envelope while opening it, but quickly gave up and tore the thing in two. Inside were several sheets of notepaper, scrawled hurriedly across in pencil. He read the letter aloud, pulling absent-mindedly at his moustache. All the key points were there: the fact that Arthur Beynon was an assumed name, and the hypothesis that it was shared by two men, probably close relatives. There was even a speculation of Irish origins, based on the sticky issue of the aitch–haitch distinction. At this, Cyril Brennan gave a choked little laugh.

'Sean was a much better performer than me, it seems,' he said, sadly. 'But if you knew this all along, why didn't you say something?'

'I thought it'd have a far greater impact coming straight from the source itself. Then, too,' said the friar, the corners of his mouth creeping skywards, 'I've always had theatrical tendencies.'

'But how did you know?' pressed Parkes.

The friar shrugged. 'I keep telling you—because it fits. And everything else I have to tell you will fit, too, but I think you'll find it much easier to believe me when we have the evidence to hand.'

Against his own better judgement, the detective sergeant relented.

'Fine,' he said. 'You've got until nightfall, but you'll have to take one of the local constables with you. I'll call for Hughes to escort you.'

'And, seeing as you've shown such a dramatic bent,' Ana put in, gently mocking, 'why don't you leave us all with a clue? That's how it's done in the detective stories, after all.'

The mendicant was delighted.

'A clue?' he said. 'Very well. It would be rather fitting, I suppose, to tell you the very first thing to arouse my suspicions. It was a painting—the painting in your dining room, in fact, Miss Harris. A bucolic little scene in oils,' he added, for the benefit of Cooper and Cyril, neither of whom had been inside the homestead at Halfwell. 'The moment I laid eyes on it, I knew that something quite unorthodox and altogether unsavoury was afoot. And with that,' he said, abruptly, 'I bid you all good day.'

Before any of them could press him further, he spun on his heel and left the library.

* * *

The detective sergeant had barely touched his lunch. The shepherd's pie sat unwanted in the centre of the table, its potato peaks and valleys hardening in the late-afternoon sun. Parkes was not alone in his lack of appetite. Ana was poking listlessly at a pile of peas and limp carrots, while Cooper and Cyril Brennan had managed about three mouthfuls between them.

It had been a little over three hours since the friar left, and to say that the time had passed pleasantly would require a comprehensive redefinition of the word 'pleasant' and all its meaningful derivatives.

Rather than descending to the crowded dining room, Parkes had asked for their food to be sent up to the balcony, the better to monitor the communications of those around him. There he hovered, hawkish, swooping in at the slightest sign of a meaningful exchange between any of the others. Whatever he had hoped to overhear—some significant slip of the tongue, perhaps, or a message in code—he was disappointed. There was no collaboration, no 'all is discovered', only the few muted niceties that etiquette demanded of a shared meal. Even alcohol, that universal lubricant, managed to lighten the mood only a little.

As glasses were emptied and refilled, the slow speculation began. Cyril led the questioning. Having now learned that Ana was, in all likelihood, the last person to see his brother alive, he was desperate for anything that might shed light on Sean's final moments.

In this, he was not alone.

The suggestion that a painting in the Harrises' own living room had a connection to the crime seemed to have awakened long-dormant suspicions anew. The significance of the artwork itself was expounded in numerous theories, ranging from the unlikely—that the scene in the painting represented the hiding place of some treasure valuable enough to kill for—to the downright ludicrous, as in Cyril's suggestion that the paint itself might contain some sort of poison, which could be flaked away and added to the tea or coffee of parched travellers in order to incapacitate them. To what end this might be done (or by whom, or how this idea intersected in any way with the fate of Sean Brennan) was not elucidated.

The detective sergeant soon tired of silent surveillance and began to pester Ana with comments and questions of his own. Even the usually reticent Cooper endeavoured to draw her into conversation, going so far as to try and take her aside when she rose to refill her sherry glass. By that time, however, the young woman had well and truly lost her patience for speculation and supposition. Abandoning the remnants of her meal, she made her excuses and, before Parkes had a chance to object, set out for her room.

She walked quickly along the carpeted corridors of the hotel, her face hot with frustration and more than a little guilt. What did the painting mean? What right did the others have to fill her home with the spectres of imagined schemes? What right did the friar have to cast the shadow of suspicion in her direction? What did he know? What *could* he know?

There was a white-hot little ember at the core of all this discomfort. A lie—well, she reasoned, more of an omission. A single element of the story that Ana had neglected to reveal to anyone. It was of a deeply personal nature, and she couldn't see how anyone would benefit from knowing about it; not the police, not the friar, and certainly not her parents. In any case, Ana was positive that it had no bearing on the murder. She had felt that from the very beginning, and each subsequent discovery had made it progressively less likely. Even so, the idea that she had withheld information would certainly not sit well with the others, and Ana had the distinct idea that everything was about to come unravelled. The friar knew something, she was certain of that much; his parting look had laid her bare.

She fairly ran up the final few steps to her room, as if the cloud of doubt and guilt might be outpaced and left at the door. Surely, she thought, slipping the latch shut behind her, the secret could have no bearing on Sean's death. It was a personal matter, and she had every right to keep it quiet. The friar would be back soon, with all his evidence, and everyone would be so relieved to have the matter put to rest that they wouldn't spare a thought for a simple little inconsistency in her story. She had only to suffer a few more hours, then the whole thing would be done, and the eyes of the world would move on to something new.

As she did in any time of heightened tension, Ana turned to her books to help her through the last fraught minutes of waiting. A dozen leather-bound worlds were waiting to offer her asylum; she had only to make her selection. She opened her trunk, reached for her book satchel and gasped.

It was gone.

She whirled through the room like a hurricane, searching for any forgotten spot in which she might have set the bag down. She stripped the bed of its covers, overturned the chairs, cast the drawers of the little writing desk carelessly to the floor, but all to no avail. Her books had not merely been misplaced; they had been taken.

She forced herself to pause a moment, stemming the rising panic. Was there anything else that had gone missing?

Her locket was still around her neck, and there was little else of value in the room. Her purse was there on the nightstand, with its meagre contents unmolested, and nothing else appeared to have been touched or moved. The only sign that anyone had entered the room at all was the neatly made bed, which Ana had now torn apart.

'The housemaid,' she hissed. Who else could the culprit have been?

Dark eyes afire with anger, she swept out of the room and down the stairs, taking them three at a time. Ever alert to the sound of running steps, the detective sergeant emerged from the corridor and threw himself into pursuit, arriving at the hotel's front desk a few breathless moments behind Ana.

She was pounding the service bell with such fury that it rapidly lost the capacity to ring, giving out instead an awful, hollow thud with each blow. The porter appeared in a wild panic, looking around for signs of a fire or a shooting. Any relief he experienced at finding nothing more than a conservatively dressed young woman was immediately obliterated when she opened her mouth.

Not knowing a word of Spanish (or indeed any language other than English), he was not privy to the actual significance of the invective hurled at him, but this did absolutely nothing to reduce its impact. Hands raised in surrender, he could do nothing but apologise indiscriminately (being unclear on the cause of the commotion) and wait for the storm to pass. The castigation could well have continued indefinitely—such was the level of frustration and anxiety fuelling Ana after the combined events of the last week—but it was finally cut short by the sudden appearance of her book satchel on the counter.

Above it was the grinning face of the mendicant.

'My apologies for having kept you all,' he said. 'Shall we reconvene upstairs?'

* * *

'I suggest we begin,' said the friar, 'by piecing together the accounts we have so far. When we have arranged what is known, the shape of what remains to be known will make itself clear.'

He surveyed his audience, assembled once again in the little library. Though the sun was now setting, the dusty old room showed no change, seemingly immune to the passage of time. The furniture had been rearranged slightly so as to create a little semicircle, at the focal point of which stood the friar, holding forth like a lecturer. Cyril leant forward in his armchair, eager to hear everything to which he had not been privy earlier. Parkes and Ana occupied the sofa, the latter still cradling her book satchel with an expression which managed to mix relief and open hostility. Cooper rounded out the group, perched on a chair brought up from the dining room. He sat stiffly, a good half a foot between his shoulders and the back of the chair, as if fearing that the whole thing would give way the moment he placed any weight upon it.

'On the night of the twenty-third of November,' the mendicant began, 'the man we now know to be Sean Brennan was riding south towards Tenindewa, just outside of Mullewa. He was travelling in the guise of Arthur Beynon, and was due to meet his brother in order to "make the switch", as it were.' He nodded to Cyril. 'Sean's route, well known to his brother, took him through the western stretches of Halfwell Station, following the path of a dry creek bed marked by a small pile of stones.

At the same time—roughly around midnight—Mariana Harris slipped out of her bedroom window and took a walk around the property. These nocturnal perambulations were occasioned, according to Miss Harris, by a desire to take in the splendour of the stars.'

The mendicant rested his gaze upon the young woman in question for several taut moments before continuing.

'When nearing the creek bed,' he said, 'Miss Harris suddenly became aware of the sound of hooves in the distance. Naturally enough for someone unexpectedly exposed in the middle of the night, she hid behind the only cover immediately available to her: the stack of stones. To her dismay, the horse seemed to be heading towards her. It drew closer, and she began to fear that she had been seen. Finally, when the hoof beats were almost upon her, she saw a flash of light—probably from an electric lantern—and heard a man yell "die".'

Cyril became the momentary focus of several sympathetic looks as the story continued.

'A commotion was heard, for the duration of which Miss Harris had her eyes tightly shut, and then Sean Brennan was lying beside her, bleeding profusely. He was either dead or very close to it. In a panic, Miss Harris ran home, telling no-one of her misadventure, and feigned ill for the whole of the following day. That night, hearing a priest (of sorts), in her dining room, she suffered an attack of conscience and crept out to show him the body.'

Clearly uncomfortable referring to himself in the third person, the friar adjusted his narrative technique. 'Before coming to see me, she went to look at the body once more. There was the chance, after all, that the whole thing had merely been a night terror, or that the man had only been injured and was in need of aid. Seeing that the man—Sean—still lay there, and that his condition would not be improving, she went to fetch me.'

From the corner of his eye, the friar saw a familiar crimson flush climb the detective sergeant's cheeks. This was the first the policeman had heard of Ana's return to the body, and his displeasure at having such a crucial element kept from him was in heated evidence. Any attempt at appeasement, the friar knew, was doomed to fail—there was nothing for it but to endure the fiery stare and forge ahead with the story.

'Meanwhile, of course, Cyril Brennan was worried. He knew Sean's schedule. It was unusual for him to be even a little late, let alone a full twenty-four hours. Under cover of darkness, he set out along the agreed route and came upon his brother's body. Grieving, he took the body with him, later deciding to remove the distinguishing clothes and dispose of it in secret—as we've all heard, he yet hoped to salvage the life they had built together, with a view to bringing the rest of the family over from Ireland. What is truly remarkable,' he said, 'is that Cyril came to collect his brother in the narrow window of time between Miss Harris first checking on the body and my returning with her, some forty minutes later.' The friar rubbed his hands together. 'And there we have it,' he said. 'The gaps in our understanding can now be seen clearly. Who was the man who yelled *die*? Why would someone want to kill Sean Brennan? And, perhaps most importantly,' he gave a significant smile, 'why did it take us so long to get to this point?'

'Because you insist on making such a show of everything,' snapped the detective sergeant. 'Stop playing at stagecraft and tell us what the painting means.'

The officer's outburst met with a low rumble of approval.

'The painting?' said the friar, mildly. 'Oh, there's nothing particularly remarkable about the painting.'

The rumble ceased to be low and no longer bore the remotest resemblance to approval. Ana looked ready to repurpose one of her treasured tomes as a missile, and Cyril gripped the arms of his chair so tightly that one of the seams began to tear. The mendicant hastened to elaborate.

'The very thing that is remarkable about the painting,' he said, hands held aloft for patience, 'is how wholly unremarkable it is, especially given that it is the only image adorning the walls of the Harris household. There are a few trinkets on the mantlepiece,' he explained, 'for the sake of Cyril and Cooper, 'and a crucifix above the door, but nothing else in the way of pictures. Doesn't that strike you as more than a little odd?' The question was addressed to the room at large.

'Consider, if you will, your own living quarters, those of your friends and family. There are photographs of the children, wedding pictures, an ancient portrait, perhaps, of Great-Aunt Mildred. The Harris household, in contrast, seems almost to invoke the Ottoman Empire, the inhabitants of which are proscribed from owning images of any human being by the tenets of their Muslim faith. Thanks to the aforementioned crucifix, we can assume that Mohammed will be little help in furnishing us with answers. What other options, then, are open to us?'

Parkes and Cyril offered a few half-plausible possibilities, but the friar's attention was fixed firmly upon Ana. Her eyes were wide and unfocussed, her lips moved without forming words. The shock, he knew, was not feigned. This line of thinking had simply never occurred to her before, and no explanation was forthcoming.

'Perhaps my next point will clarify matters somewhat,' offered the friar. 'Miss Harris has a habit of looking to her books for answers. I see no reason to break with that tradition now.'

Gently, he reached out to relieve Ana of her book satchel. She watched in a daze, making no move to stop him. The friar took a long wooden bench from along the far wall and dragged it into the centre of the room. On one side of the bench, he stacked the books from Ana's satchel.

'That some of these books have been liberated of their frontispieces has already been remarked on,' said the friar. 'Certainly not a damning thing, in and of itself. What is interesting, though,' he continued, reaching for the topmost book, 'is the pattern that emerges when we separate the intact volumes from those which have been tampered with.'

The others leant in to read the titles as the friar divided them into two distinct piles. The differences were immediately obvious. The leftmost stack comprised *Frankenstein*, several of Poe's later works, a tattered collection of Algernon Blackwood stories and Ann Radcliffe's *The Romance of the Forest*. On the right-hand side were *Rip-Roaring Adventure Tales*, a biography of Richard III, several volumes of Everyman's Poetry and Ana's Spanish primer.

'If you were to go through the shelves at Halfwell,' said the friar, 'I would hazard a guess that this pattern would continue: the books with missing pages would all be works of fiction, largely of the romantic or gothic genres. You may also notice that none of the altered books are particularly modern—certainly nothing printed in the last twenty years or so.'

'But why?' asked the detective sergeant. 'And what does it mean?'

In lieu of an answer, the friar put another question to Ana.

'Would I be correct in assuming, given your proclivities, that the birthday presents given to you by the Harrises are usually books?'

Ana nodded, the confusion on her face showing no sign of softening.

'And if, looking at all the literature assembled at Halfwell, I were to try and identify the books you had been given,' the friar continued, 'would my task be a difficult one?'

'Well, no,' she said. 'You'd simply have to look inside the front cover and find the inscription.'

The detective sergeant snapped his fingers. 'I see!' he said, with a triumphant little laugh. 'So you're suggesting that whoever removed those pages was trying to conceal their origin?'

'Or their destination,' Cyril pointed out. 'The inscription

will usually be something along the lines of: *To my dear So-and-So, best of luck for the coming year, your affectionate Aunt Whatsername.* He shook his head. 'Who on earth would need to conceal such a thing, though, and why?'

The friar smiled. 'That may become clear,' he said, 'when I have outlined the rest of my evidence. I'd like to move on, if there are no objections, to the issue of the sleeves.'

The detective sergeant blinked, nonplussed. 'Sleeves?'

'Sleeves,' said the friar. 'This particular point, I must admit, did not leap out at me immediately. It wasn't until I saw those fellows playing two-up on the train that I finally became aware of it, and even then, I struggled to grasp its full significance.'

Here, he gave a brief resumé of the two-up match, the temporary loss of the coin and its subsequent re-materialisation from within the folds of the miner's trouser cuff.

'That moment brought something into focus, something which had hitherto been bubbling away in my subconscious.' He turned towards Ana. 'Miss Harris was raised in a farming family; a famously frugal people, as a rule. It is perfectly natural, then, that she should dress in hand-me-downs. An admirable way of thinking, if you ask me. Why stitch a new frock when an old one is still perfectly serviceable? All that is needed is to make minor adjustments, letting out a hem here, taking in a collar there. Sometimes, if length is the only issue, a slight rolling or cuffing of the sleeves will suffice.'

Ana fidgeted with the cuffed sleeves of her own frock, a movement that served to instantly attract the attention of all those present.

'The question, then, is this—from whom were the clothes handed down?' The friar let the query hang for a moment. 'You will all have noticed, I trust, that Ruth Harris is several inches shorter than her adopted daughter, and though Neville Harris is a tall man, I doubt his frame would be flattered by the garments in question.' He allowed himself a wry smile. 'They could, of course, have come from outside the family, but the cut, colour and fabric are consistent with the frocks tailored and worn by Ruth Harris herself. The only other female inhabitant of the house is the serving girl, Daisy, who is smaller than the others and wears much simpler attire, and can therefore be dismissed from the equation. What remains?'

'There must have been someone else,' said Cyril, with the simple clarity of an outsider.

'Exactly,' the friar said. 'Either someone in the household, or very close to it. A woman of roughly the same build as Miss Harris, but a little longer of limb. Someone whose history at Halfwell has been concealed, or at the very least distorted.' He turned to Ana. 'I can see that this line of thinking is not a comfortable one for you, Miss Harris.'

With this assertion, the friar was forging new frontiers in understatement. Ana's fingers trembled as she toyed with her sleeves; drops of perspiration dotted her high collar. When she spoke, her voice was weak.

'Why?' she said. 'What—what does it mean?'

'It means, I believe, that there was another member of the Harris household before you,' said the friar. 'Neville and Ruth Harris have removed any pictorial or photographic evidence of her—hence the bare walls—but traces remain. And from those traces,' he continued, in the same calm, gentle voice, 'an outline can be recreated. We know, for instance, that she was a little taller than you. We know that she had a considerable appetite for fiction, with a particular taste for the romantic and the mysterious. And we know that she disappeared from the family before you were old enough to form lasting memories of her.'

Tears began to gather in Ana's eyes.

Slowly, solemnly, the friar produced a book from the pocket of his robe. It was a copy of *The Romance of the Forest*, identical to the one on the wooden bench.

'Luckily, the Fremantle library had several editions,' said the friar. 'That's why I had to take your book satchel with me—for the purposes of comparison. The moment I saw this, I knew.'

He held the book out to Ana. She stood to take it, opening the cover with trembling hands.

There was no dedication on the frontispiece, only a faded library stamp. There was, however, an illustration: a handsome, moustachioed hero, his arms around the slight waist of his adoring wife.

Ana stared. It was the same image that had lived inside her locket for so long.

The picture swam before her eyes, then all was dark.

CHAPTER SEVENTEEN

'I'm not sure I understand,' whispered Cyril. 'You're telling me that those people are her parents?'

He was hurrying back to the sofa with a bottle of brandy and a small glass. Cooper had been quick enough to catch Ana as she fainted, and was now arranging the young woman tenderly on the sofa. The detective sergeant paced awkwardly in the centre of the room.

'She was *told* that they were her parents,' said the friar, holding the liquor to Ana's lips. 'The Harrises tore that image out of the book and gave it to her, along with a rather whimsical story. All false, of course. They simply didn't want her to know the truth.'

With a fit of coughing, Ana began to come round. Cooper called for water.

'And what *is* the truth?' asked Cyril, when Ana had recovered enough to hold her own glass.

The friar hesitated, looking to Ana. Receiving permission in the form of a slight but certain nod, he reached into the pocket of his robe.

'It's a good thing you forced that constable on me,' he told Parkes. 'Without him as my escort, I doubt the town hall archivist would have let me get anywhere near this, let alone have written me out a copy.'

The blotting paper was still relatively crisp and clean. It was clear that the archivist had copied only the relevant section of a much larger document.

'It's from an Aberdeen line shipping manifest,' the friar explained, 'recorded upon arrival at the port of Fremantle.'

The document was dated July third, 1892. There were three lines of neat roundhand, each giving the details of a different passenger. Neville William Harris was listed first, along with his age, profession and liquid assets. Next was Ruth Susan Harris (née Melville), identified as the wife of the aforementioned. The final entry was Ethel Diane Harris, aged three weeks.

'Born at sea,' said the friar. 'Probably the only element of truth that the Harrises maintained in creating their false narrative.'

'You're suggesting that this is the missing member of the family?' asked the detective sergeant, stepping forward at last.

The friar nodded. 'A daughter,' he said. 'And, I believe, a mother.'

All eyes were on Ana. For almost a minute, she was unable to speak.

'Why?' she asked at last, the pain palpable in her voice. 'Why would they lie to me?'

'Not only that,' asked Parkes, 'but why would they go to such incredible lengths?' He began to count on his fingers. 'The false photograph, the new name, the Spanish lessons, the feigned adoption—it's an awful lot of effort, if you ask me.'

'Shame,' said the friar, simply.

'Shame?' Ana sobbed. 'What would they have to be ashamed of?'

'Given the size of the clothes handed down to you, we can assume that Ethel lived with her parents until adulthood, so relations must have soured after that.' The friar paused. 'I would imagine that her choice of romantic partner was the issue.'

Forgetting herself, Ana clutched at the friar's robe in hope-soaked supplication.

'Do you know who he is?' she demanded.

'I have a strong suspicion,' said the friar, gently loosening the young woman's fingers. 'It's not a difficult conclusion to arrive at, given the facts. There's something else I'd like to cover first, though.' His eyes became solemn as they met Ana's. 'In Mullewa, at the Railway Hotel, I told you that the time for honesty would come. I believe that time is at hand.'

Ana made no move to resist. She sighed heavily, looking from the friar to the detective sergeant and back again. With an absent-minded nod, she accepted a glass of water, draining it almost immediately.

'I didn't mean to lie,' she said, at last. 'I didn't mean to stretch the truth, or anything else of the sort. I was just worried—I didn't want to get her into any sort of trouble, that's all.'

'When you say "her",' the friar clarified, 'you are referring to Daisy, correct?'

Ana nodded.

'Sorry,' a confused Cyril held up a hand. 'Who the devil is Daisy?'

'She's my friend,' said Ana, impatiently. 'She works as a housemaid at Halfwell. She passed me a note, the morning before the murder. She wouldn't tell me where it came from. Someone else must've given it to her, because she can't write.'

Seeing that the detective sergeant was itching to interrupt, the friar placed a gentle hand on his chest.

'Just a minute more,' he said, before turning back to Ana. 'What did the note say?'

The young woman hesitated a moment. When she did finally speak, the words came out in a rush.

'It was about my parents,' she said. 'It said to wait by the stones at midnight if I wanted to know the truth.'

'That was all?'

'That was all. No name, no details. Daisy wouldn't tell me anything else about who gave it to her, or why. I think she might've been afraid, but it's difficult to be sure. Her English isn't very good, you see, and she's tried to teach me a bit of Wajarri, but my —' she hesitated, stumbling over her new and uncomfortable knowledge of the family history, 'the Harrises didn't like it. They used to tell us off if they heard us.'

'How did the note make you feel?'

'Well, nervous,' she sighed, fiddling with her locket. 'Anxious, I suppose, and a little excited. I was careful, though, not to take it too seriously.'

'Why?'

'Because I'd heard similar things before,' she said. 'Some of the younger stockmen used to make up stories about my parents, especially when they were bored. A couple of the children in Mullewa did, too. You know what kids are like.'

'You still decided to go to the stones at midnight, though.'

'Of course,' said Ana, simply. 'As long as there was a chance to learn more, I couldn't very well do otherwise. I wasn't lying, you know, when I said that I couldn't sleep that night. I was pacing like a mad dog all evening. Everything else I told you was true, too.'

'I don't doubt it,' the friar said. He looked to the detective sergeant. 'Well, Mr Parkes,' he yawned, stretching, 'I suppose you've heard enough to draw all the necessary conclusions.'

'Not by a long bloody shot,' snapped Parkes, furious at having to admit his ignorance. 'Wrap up your little scene, and be quick about it.'

'Very well.' The friar permitted himself a puckish chuckle before turning back to Ana. 'You know the Harrises,' he said, 'with all their prejudices and peccadilloes. What kind of partner would upset them enough to cut their own daughter out of their lives?'

Ana pondered. 'Some sort of criminal, perhaps,' she said, 'or a Protestant.'

Her little laugh was defiant in the face of looming despair.

The friar chuckled, too.

'Both of those possibilities did occur to me,' he admitted. 'In fact, they crossed my mind long before the actual answer. That is due, I suppose, to my status as a foreigner. It took me a while to familiarise myself with the lay of the cultural landscape, as it were.'

He took a moment to survey the room. The blank, impatient looks on display told him that his current line of reasoning was not being followed. He switched tracks.

'All right,' he said. 'I'll return, then, to my question of some minutes ago. Why did it take us so long to get to this point? Why did it take us so long to find Sean Brennan, and then Cyril? After all,' he went on, 'Sean's path was well used. We know that he took his horse and sulky down the same route every three months. Then, too, Cyril had just covered the same ground, collecting his brother's body only half an hour or so after Miss Harris showed me to the scene.'

The friar paused for a moment, as if gathering strength for his final push.

'How is it, then,' he said, 'that no trail was found the next day?'

He let this sink in.

'It's a remarkable fact,' he continued, 'and one that becomes all the more remarkable when the man leading the search is hailed by Detective Sergeant Parkes—someone who, I'm sure you'll all agree, is not overly prone to flattery—as the best tracker in the state.'

One by one, the listeners turned to look at Cooper.

'Not only that,' said the friar, 'but the same distinguished tracker is again unable to pick up the trail made by Cyril Brennan as he cut through the bush south of Wongoondy; terrain which, being less well trodden than the Halfwell property, should show up any disturbance with greater clarity. It's also worth noting, of course,' he threw in, casually, 'that Cooper was the person responsible for gathering evidence from the household staff—including Daisy.'

'What are you suggesting?' growled Parkes.

'I'm suggesting that the esteemed Cooper had a vested interest,' said the friar, 'in keeping the hunt running as long as possible. You will remember that he also managed to avoid identifying the sketch of Sean's face until such time as the investigation showed signs of running out of steam.'

The tracker stood stony-faced.

'But why?' the detective sergeant demanded, turning on him. 'What's in it for you?'

Cooper would not be drawn. The friar raised his hands for calm.

'I don't believe that Mr Cooper's motives were sinister,' he clarified. 'On the contrary, they could be considered altogether honourable. All of the tracker's actions, I submit, were in the interest of extending the amount of time he was able to spend beside his daughter.'

For a moment, it looked as though Ana might faint again, but she managed to catch at the arm of the sofa and hold herself upright.

'It was you, wasn't it, Mr Cooper?' said the friar, calmly. 'You were waiting by the stones that night.'

Cooper's broad chest rose and fell heavily, the only sign that he was a living being and not some sophisticated piece of statuary. Finally, after more than a minute, he gave a slow nod. All at once, the tension drained from him; relieved of his burden, he melted into the chair opposite Ana and gazed at her as if for the first time.

'I wanted to tell you,' he said. 'I *tried* to tell you—that's why I slipped Daisy the note in the first place. After everything that happened that night, though, I couldn't do anything but follow the investigation and try to get you alone. I climbed in through the hallway window at the hotel in Mullewa, but he was already knocking on your door,' he said, pointing to the friar. 'The next night, I doubled back to Wongoondy, but you were with Dawson, and I simply couldn't risk it.'

Cooper's confessions continued to pour forth, as if the previously watertight tracker had finally sprung a leak. He spoke of meeting Ethel Diane Harris for the first time. She was a boarding-school pupil in Perth, a world away from her parents in Mullewa. Though roughly the same age, Cooper had been denied the privilege of an education, and was working as an assistant to the school groundskeeper. He spoke of her quick wit, her curiosity, her adventurous spirit—how she had been one of the few girls to notice him, let alone to ask him anything about his life. Then, blinking back tears, he described how he had fallen in love with her, and she with him.

Of all the thousands of stories that Ana had been exposed to throughout her life, this was the most important. In her shock, though, she was almost beyond listening. Her world was undergoing a seismic shift, an immense upheaval. Everything upon which she had built her identity was false. None of the previous facts of her existence now held true. It defied comprehension, but it fit.

The Harrises, she knew from firsthand experience, were not the sort of people to stray from the social norm. Like so many of their neighbours, they saw the Australian continent's earliest inhabitants as wholly and unquestionably inferior to those of European descent. The thought of their only daughter having a child with a black man—even someone of mixed race, like Cooper—would have been utterly inconceivable. As far as the Harrises were concerned, it would have been entirely preferable to disavow their kinship altogether than to admit to their daughter's miscegenation. It must have been the lucky accident of Don Armando's presence in Mullewa which planted the seeds of the Chilean cover story. It was a sterling piece of misdirection, Ana had to admit, with the dual benefits of focussing her cultural curiosity elsewhere and accounting for her complexion. The more she turned it over, the more sense the whole scenario made. Only one glaring question remained unanswered.

'What happened to my mother?' she asked.

Though little more than a whisper, her voice brought the rest of the room to silence. Cooper rubbed his temples.

'When Diane found out that she was —' he hesitated, blushing absurdly. 'When she realised that she was in the family way, she went to a doctor. She made an appointment at an office in the city, on a Saturday, because she was worried that the school doctor would notify her parents. Unfortunately, this city fellow did exactly the same thing, only he didn't tell her he was going to do it—the Harrises turned up without warning two days later and took her straight from the school.' Tears began to find their way over his cheeks. 'I didn't even get a chance to say goodbye. I didn't know then—about you, I mean. It was weeks before her friends finally told me what they'd all been whispering about in the days before Diane's disappearance. None of them knew exactly where the Harrises' station was—at least, no-one who was willing to tell me—but I knew they couldn't have been far from Geraldton. We grew up on the same country, Diane and I. She used to tell me how she missed the everlastings. So as soon as I could get back up north, I started to search for them. For her. For you. I never stopped.'

Cooper drew a long, shuddering breath, holding his daughter's gaze. 'You look exactly like your mum,' he said at last, low and gentle. 'I always told myself I'd get to you. One day, when you were ready. For years, I gathered little bits of gossip, little bits of news from people in passing. I heard about you starting Sunday school. I heard you collected books, and that you loved the stars, just like she did. Out by the stones, when that light flashed over your face, and I saw you for the first time —' he sighed. 'It was the happiest moment of my life.

Everything was worth it, all those years of waiting. I couldn't believe it. I couldn't contain myself —'

'And you cried out the name of the woman you thought you were seeing,' the friar finished, smoothly.

There was a moment of shocked silence.

'Di!' growled the detective sergeant from behind his moustache. 'Not *die*, but *Di!*'

Cooper nodded.

'Her first name was Ethel, but she never liked it—thought it was too old-fashioned—so she went by Diane. I always called her Di.'

'By an unhappy coincidence,' said the friar, 'you called out just as Sean Brennan was passing. He had kept to the back ways, as usual, looking for the stones to get his bearings.'

Cyril let loose a sob. 'That must've spooked the horse,' he said, clutching at his hair. 'She was skittish at the best of times.'

'Are you suggesting,' said Parkes, 'that there was no murder at all? That Sean was simply thrown by a nervous horse and happened to hit his head on a rock?'

'That's the conclusion to which the facts have led me,' the friar nodded. 'Tragic, certainly—somehow both rather mundane and a little unlikely—but I think you'll find it to be the only explanation that fits all the evidence.'

The men in the room began to mutter all at once, swept up in the solution. They turned it over to examine from all angles, dissecting it like a particularly impressive sporting play. Only Ana was unaffected.

'You still haven't answered my question,' she said, to the room at large. 'What happened to my mother? Where is she now?'

The discussion ceased. Cooper shook his head.

'I don't know,' he admitted. 'I think the only people who will be able to tell us the truth are Neville and Ruth Harris. I've spent years looking through records offices, convents, cemeteries —'

'Cemeteries?' interrupted Ana. 'You think she's dead, then?'

Cooper hesitated. 'I think it's likely,' he said, at last. 'I haven't seen any sign of her, and there are plenty of things that can go wrong in childbirth, especially out there —'

Before he could finish, Ana was gone. This final blow had proved too much. Not bothering to hide her tears, she ran for the door.

* * *

The friar found Ana on the balcony, gazing out at the darkening sky.

If she heard the creak of his footsteps on the weather-warped boards, she gave no sign. Wordlessly, he padded up to take his place alongside her on the railing. The half-moon hung above them, struggling to be seen against the glow of the harbour lights. For a very long time, neither of them spoke.

'I suppose you've known all along, haven't you?' said Ana, at last. Her eyes remained fixed on the horizon.

'About Cooper?' the friar exhaled slowly. 'No, I must admit, it took me quite a while to figure that one out. You're right, though, that my suspicions about your origins were aroused from the very beginning.'

He produced a book from the seemingly bottomless pockets of his cassock.

'When I first heard your name, I was reminded of something, but it wasn't until I got to the library this afternoon that I was finally able to verify it.' He tapped the book against the balustrade. 'I asked you once if you had read Cervantes. This is a copy of his *Novelas Ejemplares*. It's in translation, of course, but your family names appear to have been borrowed from the protagonist of one of the stories—*La Gitanilla*.'

Ana turned. '*The Little Gypsy Girl*,' she said, reaching for the book. 'Must have been someone's idea of a joke.' She flipped through the pages, scanning the faded ink for her own plagiarised persona. 'Here it is. Constanza de Azevedo y de Meneses,' she sighed, handing the book back. 'It could have been much worse, I suppose. Her given name is Preciosa.'

There was a lull in the conversation. Snatches of song and revelry floated up from the public house below.

'They'll probably try to tell me they did the right thing,' said Ana. 'My family, I mean. Maybe they even believe it themselves. They didn't want me to be treated the way they treat Aboriginal people. The idea of changing their own beliefs, though, was evidently far more daunting than the idea of changing me.'

'Are you going to confront them?' asked the friar.

'I have to,' Ana said. 'If I ever want to know what really happened to mother, I simply don't have a choice.'

'And what of your father?'

Ana shook her head a little, at a loss to explain the enormity before her.

'He needs you,' said the friar, earnestly. 'He's spent a lifetime—your lifetime—searching for you. He needs to know that it means something.'

'Of course it means something,' Ana's voice quivered a little. 'How could it not? I just—I've got no idea what to say to him. Everything's changed so quickly. I don't know what to think. I don't know how to think about myself, let alone anyone else.'

'That's natural. All will come right with time. Unfortunately,' the friar said, 'time may not be as plentiful as we might hope.'

Ana looked up in alarm.

'What do you mean?' she demanded.

'The detective sergeant is in deliberations as we speak. He is none too pleased, I believe, with the idea of having been deceived by an underling. There is also the question,' the friar pointed out, 'of who is culpable for the death of Sean Brennan.'

'But it was an accident!'

'True,' said the friar, 'but we have arrived at this knowledge only after unravelling a knot of obfuscations and mistruths.

Parkes will want to allay his own suspicions with further investigation. He has also made it clear that lying to the authorities is not generally viewed in a particularly favourable light. This transgression, unfortunately, is one of which all of us —you, Cooper, Brennan and myself—are guilty.'

'What can we do?' asked Ana.

The friar smiled.

'I fear that I have already done altogether too much,' he said, 'and I doubt the esteemed officer will give me any more of his time. He might be more willing to listen to you, though, especially on the issue of Cooper.' He reached out to take Ana's hand. 'Stand with your father. Show that all this awful deception may yet be in aid of something good. Perhaps the promise of some joy to be gained from all this sorrow will soften the detective sergeant's heart.'

Ana hesitated a moment, then shook her head. 'I wouldn't know what to say,' she said.

The friar regarded her closely. 'I've never known you to be lost for words,' he said.

For nearly a minute, Ana gazed out over the port city. A guttering breeze blew in from the ocean, sharp with salt.

'I'm worried,' she said, finally. 'I'm worried that Coo—' she caught herself. 'That my father will be disappointed.' She sighed. 'He must have built an image in his head, over all those years of searching; the child he hoped for, the child of his first and only love. How can I live up to that? What am I? *Who* am I? I don't even have my own name anymore. Shall I become a Cooper?' Her eyes widened. 'That can't be my father's real name, either. I doubt his mother called him Cooper. My grandmother, I mean. My *other* grandmother. Oh, God!' she cried. 'It's all too much!'

The friar took her firmly by the shoulders.

'Look at me,' he said. He waited for her eyes to find his. 'The simple fact that you care is enough, that you're trying to see the world through the eyes of another.' He gave a self-deprecating smile. 'I can't give you much in the way of life wisdom, I'm afraid—you've seen enough of me to know that I'm just as foolish as the next man. What I can tell you, though, is that if you care at all about others, you've got to look after yourself first. It may not make much sense at first, but if you don't know yourself, you'll be no good to anyone. I can also tell you that knowing yourself has nothing to do with your name. If anyone knows that,' he grinned, 'it's me. I know who I am, now. When I left England, I didn't just run from prosecution or punishment; I ran from the truth in my own heart. I shan't run again. I know who I am.'

Ana couldn't help but smile back at the strange little man. She held his gaze a moment.

'If that's true,' she said, with a hint of mischief in her voice, 'you'll have no trouble telling me your name. After all, I know you, don't I?'

For a fraction of a second, the old fear shone in the friar's eyes. Then, recognising the trap as one of his own making, he laughed.

'It would seem that you know me very well indeed,' he said, and told her his name.

Ana took his hand.

'Pleased to meet you,' she said. 'And my name is Mariana Harris—at least for now.'

ACKNOWLEDGEMENTS

My eternal gratitude goes out to everyone who made this book possible.

To the team at Fremantle Press, especially Georgia Richter, who helped to bring my story to life with passion, humour and attention to detail.

To Marisa Wikramanayake, whose historical insights, eye for punctuation and editing finesse helped iron out the wrinkles in my manuscript.

To Mum and Dad, for their lifelong support, from reading to me as a child to proofreading for me thirty years later.

To Grandpa, whose stories of growing up all over the country provided my tale with context and colour.

To Grayson, whose engineering expertise was put to good use answering questions about the buoyancy of fictional objects.

To all those who read extracts, went through early drafts and provided me with general encouragement: Jordan, Kris, Sarah S, Sarah R, Ling, Margaret, Maureen, Aunty Wendy and Aunty Al. Finally, to Lindsay, who lifts me up and gives love unreservedly, and without whom I would be lost.

ABOUT THE AUTHOR

Alexander Thorpe grew up in the suburbs to the south of Perth, Western Australia. He has written about the virtues of artificial turf as an advertising copywriter, explored the fringes of the former Soviet Union as an English teacher and accidentally sealed his own feet in concrete during a blissfully brief stint as a construction hand. When not writing, Alexander can be found inflicting his idiosyncratic brand of English on innocent students, exploring new frontiers in miserable music or embracing his insomnia in the company of an old British radio drama. *Death Leaves the Station* is his first novel.

Cryogenicist Dr Georgette Watson has mastered the art of bringing frozen hamsters back to life. Now what she really needs is a body to confirm her technique can save human lives—and fate and family connections are about to come to her aid.

Meanwhile, in New York City, winter is closing in and there's a killer on the loose, slaying strangers who seem to have nothing in common. Is it simple good fortune that Georgette, who freelances for the NYPD, suddenly finds herself in the company of the greatest detective of all time? And will Sherlock Holmes be able to crack the crimes in a world that has changed drastically in two hundred years, even if human nature has not?

THE
EDWARD STREET
BABY FARM
STELLA BUDRIKIS
THE MURDER TRIAL THAT GRIPPED A CITY

In 1907, Perth woman Alice Mitchell was arrested for the murder of five-month-old Ethel Booth. During the inquest and subsequent trial, the state's citizens were horrified to learn that at least thirty-seven infants had died in Mitchell's care in the previous six years. It became clear that she had been running a 'baby farm', making a profit out of caring for the children of single mothers and other 'unfortunate women'.

The Alice Mitchell murder trial gripped the city of Perth and the nation. This book retraces this infamous 'baby farm' tragedy, which led to legislative changes to protect children's welfare.

First published 2020 by
FREMANTLE PRESS

Fremantle Press Inc. trading as Fremantle Press
25 Quarry Street, Fremantle WA 6160
(PO Box 158, North Fremantle WA 6159)
www.fremantlepress.com.au

Cover images are from www.shutterstock.com: Ensuper, javarman,
ninanaina, TABITO_EX, Piter Kidanchuk.
Printed by McPherson's Printing, Victoria, Australia.

 A catalogue record for this
book is available from the
National Library of Australia

ISBN 9781925816006 (paperback)
ISBN 9781925816013 (ebook)

Fremantle Press is supported by the State Government through
the Department of Local Government, Sport and Cultural Industries.

Publication of this title was assisted by the Commonwealth Government
through the Australia Council, its arts funding and advisory body.